STRANGERS TO TEMPTATION

STRANGERS
to
TEMPTATION

stories

SCOTT GOULD

HUB CITY PRESS
SPARTANBURG, SC

The following stories have been previously published, and a number have appeared in different form: "Bases," in the *Kenyon Review*, as well as the anthologies *New Stories from the South* and *New Southern Harmonies*; "Orbit" and "Stand-In Jesus," in *Carolina Quarterly*; "You Dream, You Leave," in *Crescent Review* as "Out of Town"; "Watching," in *St. Andrews Review;* "The Esso Trifecta," in the *Raleigh Review* as "Collection Day Is Saturday"; "Joy to the World" in *Eclectica* as "Hammer, Anvil and Stirrup"; "Matthewmarklukeandjohn" in *Pembroke Magazine* as "Strangers to Temptation"; "Bodies That Drift in the River Flow" in the *New Ohio Review.*

Book Design: Meg Reid
Cover Illustration: Maggie Chiang
Proofreaders: Meredith Hardwicke & Beverly Knight
Printed in Dexter, MI by Thomson-Shore

Library of Congress Cataloging-in-Publication Data
Gould, Scott, 1959- author.
Strangers to temptation : stories by Scott Gould.
Spartanburg, S.C. : Hub City Press, 2017.
LCCN 2016036211 | ISBN 9781938235306
Subjects: LCSH: Teenage boys—Fiction. | Small cities—Fiction. | City and town life—Fiction.
LCC PS3607.O8936 .A6 2017 | DDC 813/.6—dc23
LC record available at https://lccn.loc.gov/2016036211

HUB CITY PRESS
186 West Main St.
Spartanburg, SC 29306
1.864.577.9349
www.hubcity.org
www.twitter.com/hubcitypress

For Jack Gould.
And in memory of his bride, Mary Ann.

CONTENTS

ORBIT

I WAS THIRTEEN, AND I WATCHED LONNIE TISDALE HANDLE his fake eyeball on more than one occasion. It was an act more miraculous than grotesque, at least at that age—an ability that seemed a generous reward for all the pain he'd had to endure because of the refrigerator. Practically everybody in Kingstree knew better than to jump off Baker's Bridge in summer. The heat always shrank the Black River and raised its banks, and we were aware of the appliances and rusted transmissions and angle iron there, just under the surface of the cola-colored water. From above, you couldn't see anything below. The water was way too dark and the bridge a little too high. So we always waited until after a good rain to jump. Lonnie's impatience overcame his good sense one afternoon that summer, and he took a Kenmore to the right side of his head.

After the surgery to put his face back together, my mother refused to let me visit Lonnie. She said it would upset me, but my mother's subtext was that Lonnie's stupidity might be contagious. She was a nurse. She knew better. But she also knew Lonnie did things that brought him within a gnat's hair of death. He was the boy who hung between the trestle rails when the lumber train ran through town on its way to the paper mill. He was the boy who snuck up on alligators sleeping across the hot sand bars on Black River. Now he was the boy who had fake bones in his face. He was a hero.

I heard about the plastic side of his face long before I ever saw it. My mother came back from her shift at the hospital with daily reports of his progress. "Well, it's too swollen to tell what it's going to look like," she said one afternoon. "One half of his face looks, frankly, like a buttocks cheek." I had never heard my mother mention any body part that was covered most of the time. I suppose she saw enough orifices and fleshy parts at the hospital, she didn't want to think about more of them at the dinner table. A week later, the butt check had subsided. "Lonnie got his false eye today," she told me in a voice that sounded too celebratory, the same voice you might use to announce the winner of a church raffle.

To be honest, I had stopped thinking about Lonnie Tisdale on a regular basis. When you're thirteen, tragedy is a passing annoyance. Lonnie's recovery was something I couldn't see, so I didn't consider it important enough to catalog in my head. I was busy with Laurice Reeves.

She was the girl closest to being a boy that I knew, and I was sure I loved her. I'm relatively confident this was no latent homoeroticism lurking in my bones, but rather the fact I coveted a female who could fish and blow smoke rings. On the seventh grade playground, she wore t-shirts with nothing else on underneath and leather gloves she stole from her mother.

She'd cut the fingers out of the gloves and during recess, she pretended to be riding a large motorcycle. On one thin forearm was an ink tattoo, a design she freshened every day with an ancient-looking fountain pen. It depicted a coiled rattlesnake and some writing: *Take no crap from any man woman or child.* I'm not sure how she avoided the principal's office with *crap* on her arm and no bra under her shirt, but none of our teachers (women who could detect the rustle of a passing note at thirty feet) noticed either. I loved Laurice because I was scared of her. I wasn't the only one. But my fortunate advantage was she lived down the street from me, nearer Highway 52. In summers, I passed her house on the way to the Bantam Chef when my mother or father left money on the kitchen counter for cheeseburgers.

We never knew exactly where my father went the times he disappeared. He didn't have a job because he couldn't work. He said his stomach wouldn't allow it. His stomach was a daily source of drama and conversation when he was around, because he'd lost a sizeable chunk of it right after his return from Vietnam. A sneaky Southeast Asian parasite set up shop in his gut, and a doctor in San Francisco removed half the stomach. I told my little brother that when our father was gone, he was off searching for his missing stomach, and this gave Eli nightmares for years. Our father would go AWOL for two days and return with a spackling bucket full of redbreast and we'd say, *Ah, fishing.* He'd come back with a black eye and a gash across the bridge of his nose and we'd say, *Ah, fighting.* Sometimes he would come back after a week and wouldn't say a word, and we didn't know what to ask. Neither did our mother. It was just the way it was then.

So Lonnie was still in the hospital. My father was fishing or fighting or swallowing his tongue somewhere. My mother was working double-shifts at Kelly Memorial, which meant Eli and I spent most of the week riding our bikes back and forth to the Bantam Chef for food. We'd pedal by Laurice's house, riding with no hands on the handlebars, carrying our burgers and orange sodas. I steered with my hips. I remember that week being so hot, I felt my bike tires sink into the gooey asphalt. We had to pedal harder under the sun.

Every afternoon, I begged for Laurice to be in her yard or on her porch. The day she yelled at me, I wasn't sure where the voice came from. It just happened on the air.

"That crap will kill you," she said, the voice hovering in the trees or the azalea bushes. I thought, *Crap must be her favorite word. I should remember that.* Eli didn't hear a thing because he was hungry. He kept pedaling for home. I sometimes thought his ever-increasing appetite was compensation for my father, who seemed to live on grains of rice and ginger ale, at least when he was home.

I stopped before I was ready, backpedaled on the brake before I rearranged the things in my hands, and my soda fell to the pavement, leaving an orange puddle under my bike. "Best thing that could have happened to you," she said, dropping from her hiding spot in the thick magnolia limbs. I started to ask her why she was in a tree, but she answered before I could speak. "I'm watching people. I'm not hiding or anything," she said. "You guys go to the Bantam Chef couple times a day, don't you?"

"My mom's working," I told her. "She's a nurse." Laurice had on shorts that didn't fit her. Her legs had grown since school let out. She was taller than I'd remembered. And she was tan in every place I looked, like she'd been to the beach for a month.

"Wait here," she said and ran into her house. It wasn't a big place, but it was solid-looking, cement blocks painted a light green, an odd-angled roof, a porch without a screen on it. The front door made metal noises when it opened and closed.

Laurice ran back out with a bottle of Orange Crush in her hand. "Here," she said, "don't drop this one."

"I thought this stuff is going to kill me," I said.

"What don't?" she told me and climbed back into the magnolia. My breath caught low in my throat while I watched her legs disappear into the thick canopy of summer leaves.

LONNIE CAME HOME from the hospital on a Wednesday morning. He rode his bicycle to my house the same afternoon. Before he even sat down, he told me he wanted to show me something that would make me puke. He wanted to bet me five dollars I'd throw up the second I saw it. I wouldn't take the bet, but that didn't stop Lonnie.

"Here's the thing," he said. "That doctor who put my face together said I had to keep my new eyeball clean. I mean, not my eyeball, but the socket part." Lonnie leaned toward me so his face would catch some light. The swelling that my mother told me about was pretty much gone. I could see the thin tracks of fresh scars dividing his face into sections. He was puffy on the curve of his jaw and his eye looked a little too big for his face, the fake eye, I mean. And the fake eye never moved. It just stared straight ahead, even when Lonnie shook his head. Still, he looked mostly like Lonnie, except one side of his expression never changed. He was slightly lopsided.

"The doctor told me, 'You don't keep it clean, Lonnie, you'll get infected,' and the last thing I need is infection, you know?" He pointed to his eye to punctuate the importance of a clean socket.

"So," Lonnie continued, "they give me these little wipey things I'm supposed to use." He reached into his pocket and pulled out a small plastic sleeve of wet tissues. Then he popped his fake eye out. He rolled it carefully between two fingers like a round diamond. He smiled.

"This doesn't make me want to puke," I said, which surprised me. I normally didn't enjoy gazing on anything associated with pain. But to be honest, Lonnie's fake eye looked more like a carnival trinket than a body part.

"Eyeball. Big deal, right?" he said, laying it carefully in a crack on my den table so it wouldn't roll away. "The big deal is where it came from."

Lonnie cocked his head toward me. The hole in his head wasn't exactly black. A pinkish flap of skin stretched across the back of the opening. It was as if somebody in the vicinity of his brain had lit a candle. His socket glowed right in front of my eyes. With two fingers, he pried the opening wider. I could see the milky plastic of the rebuilt eye socket. Lonnie gagged a little, trying to talk.

"What?" I said, looking down at the table.

Lonnie cleared his throat. "Trying to say, something went wrong with my palate. Don't ask me what. They left a hole and they didn't know I could get my tongue up in there. They want to close it up one day. Hell with that. I can almost stick my tongue in my own eye. Check it out," he said. And he may have said something else, but I missed it. Instead of listening, I ran for the back porch and made it in time to throw open the screen and puke across the azalea bushes.

"Nice shot," my father said, standing there, his worn-out Army OD bag at his feet, looking like a skinny Jesus with his hair and beard and sandals. By the time Lonnie walked out, the eye was back in his head, and he wore a crooked grin over the good half of his face.

IT NORMALLY TOOK my father about two minutes to ease back into the family mode when he returned from one of his excursions. It took longer for my mother. She had to hate him awhile before she decided to love him again. He never gave her much information when she demanded details. His stock answer was, There's not much to tell, *hon.* When my mother peeled the fried skin away from a chicken breast and offered it to him, that's when we knew it was safe to breathe again.

That night, after my mother walked in to find her husband home, after she interrogated him in the hall and he said a dozen times that there was nothing to tell, hon, we sat at the table and gave thanks over a bucket of chicken from the Bantam Chef. "Dear Lord," my father said to the ceiling, "thank you for my safe return. Thank you for Lonnie Tisdale's new face—"

"And eye socket," Lonnie interrupted.

"That too. And thank you for family," he said, dropping his gaze to the bucket. "Y'all go ahead. I don't have much of an appetite."

My mother said, "*God* knows where you were. He sees it all, you know." This was a new tactic. My mother normally left God out of arguments.

"We got an agreement," my father said.

"You and God?" Lonnie asked, impressed.

"He gets decent prayers and I get left alone. I might have me a splash of that brown gravy," he said. My dad's stomach could handle soupy things, but not solid chicken. He'd end up rolling on the floor, grabbing at his sides if he ate so much as a couple bites of anything with substance.

"I thought about God when I was in the hospital. Probably thought about him when I was under the water, but I don't remember that," Lonnie said with his mouth full. As a matter of fact, Lonnie didn't recall climbing up on the bridge scaffolding and diving into the black water. He said when he woke up in the hospital, it was like someone had pulled the ultimate practical joke on him—dressed him up in a gown and ripped half his smile off.

My dad studied the bad side of Lonnie's face. "Trauma will always bring religion into the picture," he said. "God was a regular in Vietnam." Any mention of Vietnam meant war stories were close behind. My mother's eyebrow arched a little. She knew. My father's Vietnam stories constantly centered on Asian parasites and foot rot, as though the entire conflict had taken place inside of a smelly sock. We were never sure *he* was sure who the real enemy was. My mother tried to cut off the approaching tales of leper-like toes and microbes in canteens.

"Did you pray in the hospital?" she asked Lonnie.

He thought for a second. "I suppose you might call it that," Lonnie said. "What I did was make a list of all the things I better get done because you never know when you might jump into a refrigerator."

"Carpe diem," my father said.

"No, a Kenmore," Lonnie said back.

"No, I mean—never mind," my father said, staring at the bucket of chicken and breathing heavily, as though he were eating through his nostrils. My mother spooned another scoop of gravy on his paper plate, in lieu of real meat. She worked hard always to keep him distracted, if not happy.

"That's a very mature concept," my mother said, bending her head toward me as if to suggest I should take note of Lonnie's wisdom and ambition.

"Well, lose your eye and everything looks different," Lonnie said as though he'd been rehearsing the line, said it before I could mention to my mother that Lonnie Tisdale had been, for as long as I could remember, so full of shit, he'd float, which in actuality may have saved his life the day he lost an eye.

LATER THAT EVENING, just after Lonnie left and before the bats came out to chase the last of the mosquitoes, I rode to Laurice's house to watch her in her window. Thinking about it now, I can't recall if I realized how creepy and desperate it was—to leave my bike in the hedges near her mailbox and belly-crawl through the azaleas to a low spot in her yard, where I could see everything I needed and not be spotted in the shadows. I spied for the reason anybody spies: to find out something nobody knows you know. Secret information is the best kind. It gives you an upper hand, even if you never play it. Spying on Laurice wasn't sexual. I was more curious than anything. I wanted to catch her in a moment that might be described as intimate, without her realizing I was right there with her.

Laurice's parents watched television. They didn't move their heads or their mouths, the screen's glow shifting across their faces like an eclipse. Laurice, on the other hand, was all energy and movement in the bedroom above them. She sang, she danced, she called people on the white phone in her room. Once her father yelled toward the ceiling, to tell her to quiet down or quit doing the Pony on her floor, I guess, but she didn't stop until Lonnie came to the door.

I knew what carpe diem meant, even if Lonnie Tisdale didn't. It meant not wasting time. It meant doing things without thinking too much about them. It meant calling Laurice Reeves and showing up at her doorstep the day you got out of the hospital. Laurice was one of the things Lonnie thought about while the buttock cheek on his face quit swelling and his stitches dried up. Lying there in the pine straw, with no doubt a few hundred families of red bugs invading my waist, I learned that just because you love somebody secretly, she doesn't go off the market. This knowledge continues to sledgehammer me about twice a year, not matter how old I get.

They sat on the porch like high school kids on a date, the only light from the closest windows and the streetlight at the curb. I could see Laurice's mother spying on them from the den window, which I thought was pretty awful and deceitful, until I remembered I was no better. When Laurice wasn't giggling or pointing at Lonnie's face, she covered her cheeks, probably in horror from the stories he told her, stories about sunken Kenmores and black water and fake eyes. She didn't seem to act quite like herself.

After a bit, Laurice stood up. I thought she was leaving him, but instead she ducked inside the door and turned on the harsh overhead porch light. Though I couldn't make out what they said to each other, I could see better now. Lonnie popped out his fake eye and rolled it in his palm. With his other hand, he pointed to his empty socket. Laurice peered closer, then suddenly shrieked. Lonnie laughed. Laurice leaned in a second time and Lonnie repeated the show more than once. I could tell—Laurice loved seeing whatever might show up in the eye socket. From where I lay, she didn't appear to be a girl who would puke. I saw Lonnie reach in his pocket. He opened his wallet and took out a bill. I'm guessing it was a five to cover a bet he just lost.

LIVE LONG ENOUGH. You'll look back and regret your collection of tiny moments when you turned left and should have gone right, when events—cosmic or otherwise—conspired for or against you. (*If I'd caught one more light, I would never have been t-boned by that pickup at Main and Stone Avenue...*) I had one of those with Lonnie. I avoided him for a week. It was easy. He was, as I mentioned, a local hero, and he had no time to wonder why I didn't call him to go fishing, or why I never rode my bike to his house. His picture was in the *Kingstree Times*. Boy Scout Troop 17, under the leadership of Mr. Sprinkle, created a special merit badge honoring Lonnie (which was, incidentally, in the shape of a fiery eyeball.) I was easily forgotten for a week.

But I was there every night, lying in the pine straw, watching Laurice's mother watch her daughter and Lonnie. Every night, he showed her the empty orbit of his eye. Every night, she shrieked and asked for more. Then one night, when Laurice's mother finally gave up her spot at the den window and Lonnie put his eyeball back in the socket, Laurice leaned over and kissed him. Lonnie ran his hand up Laurice's t-shirt and she didn't move an elbow to block him. She didn't seem to mind where his hands were going or where his tongue had been.

I wanted to leave but they would have heard me rustling through the azalea bushes. And I wanted to yell at Lonnie, wanted to say that just because he only possessed a single eye, he was nothing special. But he was. He was a boy who gave Death the finger, and women will always love men who defy mortality. But I didn't realize that then. I only knew that I felt cheated by a boy with one eye.

When the lights went out and Lonnie left for home, I pedaled through the neighborhood. I had no concept, at thirteen, of therapy, yet I somehow sensed talking to another person would be healthy. My father was the smartest person I knew. He could help me. I needed explanations, and he never lacked for answers to anything, unless my mother asked the questions. When I got home, I found my mother sitting in the dark in the living room. The only time anyone went into our living room was at Christmas (because that's where we put the tree) or when my father left. This was August. He'd gone again, chasing his appetites.

I should have been smart enough to recognize this wasn't a good time. In the half-light from the hall, I could see she had a glass, and I smelled the orange Tang. My mother only drank when my father left and then, only Tang and Smirnoff. Now, she sat, staring, as if she were trying to figure out a math problem in her head.

"He's gone again," I said, making sure it didn't sound like a question.

"Naturally," she said. I heard ice cubes crackle in the glass.

I told her I needed to ask her something and she didn't answer. "It's important. I would've asked Dad, but—," I said. I heard her let go of a breath. She rarely cried. I blamed that on her job at the hospital. She probably saw enough crying there. Instead of tears, my mother sighed when she was upset, letting air and a tiny moan escape her mouth at the same time.

"Well, asking your father for help," she said. "Not such a good plan, eh, *hon?*"

"I like Laurice," I said. Now that I think of it, she was already aware of this. I wasn't giving her anything new. Down the hall, I heard the television break into music of some kind, something loud my brother was watching.

"Congratulations," she said, "your medal is in the mail." I heard the ice in her glass shift. Her sarcasm increased with every sip of Tang and Smirnoff.

"Never mind," I said and started to walk toward the hall.

"Wait," she said quickly. "I'm not good with boy stuff. I'm probably not the one to give you ideas right now. They'll be bad ones."

"It's okay," I said. "I don't think she likes me anyway. She likes Lonnie. He keeps showing her his eye. And they kiss a lot. I don't get it."

My mother appeared at the edge of the shadows and stood in front of me. She still wore her nurse's whites, but her shoes were off. She looked like a ghost, a very tired one. She reached forward with her hand, the one without the glass and patted me on the head like I was the family dog. It's one of the few times I remember her hand on me.

"I don't know whether this will make you feel better or worse," she said, "but here's the deal. You will never get

it. Ever. So if you give up trying, nobody will blame you."
She took a step toward the hall, into the brighter light, then
stopped when an idea struck her. "Or," she said, "or it could
be that you can't trust a man who's missing something." She
sighed right when she said that.

I'VE NEVER FIGURED out what it was about being thirteen,
the way you think you're the core of every existing universe,
the way any event that happens to you is epic and mythic, the
most important thing that will ever occur. My father was off
again, drinking or scrapping and telling Vietnam stories about
sipping bad water from a rice paddy and losing half a stomach—and he'd be back only when he was too hungry or too
lonely. My mother was mixing astronaut juice and vodka in
the kitchen and sighing, probably wondering if we would be
able to feed ourselves if she up and left and disappeared forever
in her nurse's whites, like a ghost on a mission. But when you
are thirteen, none of the drama orbiting around you matters,
especially when your one-eyed friend has his hand up your
girlfriend's shirt. (Even if she never knew she was your girlfriend.) And you *make* yourself watch it. The world became
very small in that moment, too tiny to hold any more than me
and the two people on Laurice's front porch.

If my mother heard me crack the front door and ease out,
she didn't say a word to stop me. The last thing I heard was the
theme music from some show on the television when I walked
into the thick night-air on the porch. It smelled old outside, as
if the air had gone stale. I could have done a half-dozen things
to make that night pass, could have eaten leftover chicken or

messed with my little brother or snuck back to my room and jerked off with the picture of Miss December that Lonnie stole from his father's night table and gave to me. Anything except climb on my bicycle and ride into the dark. I didn't go fast, but still, when I hit the pools of lights under the telephone poles, the moths pelted me like soft bullets as I glided through them.

Instead of heading toward Laurice's house and the Bantam Chef, I went left—not right—toward the river. The streetlights gave up, and the cicadas sang louder the closer I rode to the furniture store. I felt the slight downgrade as I came off the bluff and coasted toward the flood plain. The security light from Baker's Furniture Store glowed near their loading dock, fuzzy in the humidity, giving me just enough light to find the beginning of the sidewalk at the end of the bridge. I left my bike in the weeds. What little glow there was made the bridge shine white, like it was covered in ice, which confused me for a quick second until I realized how hard I was sweating from the ride. I reminded myself it was the end of August. We hadn't felt rain in weeks. I heard the river gurgle as it dodged the thick cement footings somewhere under me. I found a place to balance on the rail. We're all idiots when we're thirteen. All I had to do was take that step into nothing but the invisible, heavy air.

Complete idiots. We think the world cares when we're thirteen. I don't really recall all that happened next, but I knew below me was only water, and under that, things I would never be able to see, and as it turned out, none of it killed me.

BASES

BACK THEN, THERE WERE ALWAYS TWO, MAYBE THREE black boys on the other side of the tracks that ran alongside the first base line. The tracks were raised above the field on a steep hill, so they would lie flat against the slope, waiting for the train to come through on its way from the lumber mill. When it did, they would lob rocks at us from behind the steady rush of cars, and we'd run to our dugouts until the caboose passed by and the man in the window waved. By then, of course, the black boys would be nowhere in sight. The umpire would holler and start things up, and as soon as we picked the rocks out of the field, we would be baseball players again. In the stands, the people—mostly mothers and fathers—sat and looked over their shoulders at the tracks, in the direction of Nicholtown, where all the black people lived. It was just something that happened.

One afternoon, early in the game, we were already way ahead. I could smell the creosote railroad ties cooling down after a day in the sun. Someone had turned the lights on. I could hear the bulbs buzzing above the field. The train blew a warning at the far end of town, so some of the parents stood up and tried to wave us off the field before any of us even saw the locomotive.

Be smart, they were saying to us. Get off that field before you have to make a run for it. We grinned and waved back and acted like big leaguers. We spit pink bubblegum juice in the dust and chattered at the kid standing at home plate.

The locomotive churned behind first base. We knew we could probably get in a couple more pitches before the rocks started. The noise from the train spun everything into a kind of dream. Mouths moved, but the only sound was the clank and groan of the cars on the rails. The umpire jerked up his arm and screamed, but you couldn't hear the call. Parents tried to yell at their boys. Then, it started.

Our third baseman ran by. "Niggers." He mouthed the word carefully against the noise from the tracks.

The rocks fell in lazy, heavy arcs, so slow you could dodge them easily as you ran to the dugout. I headed in from short-stop, kept my eyes up, and saw the caboose pass by. Short train. Less time for them to throw. That was good for the slower guys, the dumber ones who couldn't run and watch the sky at the same time.

But above us on the rails, in the fumes the train left behind, was one of the black boys in full sight. He was big, and stood facing us, cocked up a little on one hip, his arms at his sides. He peered down into the field for a second, then began his windup from his huge pitcher's mound.

High leg kick.

Push off.

I saw the exact second the rock left his hand, and I watched his pitch spin through the air. It had no arc. Just a steady, straight line from the tracks to the field. I could almost hear the rock when it hissed over the dugout and caught Cal, our first baseman, in the face, on his cheek. Cal flopped across the foul line in the clay dust. The boy on the tracks flipped us the bird and jumped out of sight.

CAL'S MOTHER WAS on her hands and knees in the base path, looking at the ground, but screaming at us. "What are you gonna do!" she yelled. "Somebody?" She was too stocky to be crawling around in the dirt in a dress.

Most of us were a few feet away, keeping her at a safe distance as though she had a disease. But right beside her, our coach balanced Cal like a drunk, holding him up by his collar. Cal didn't know where he was, but he could mumble and sort of stand up, blood running from the cut on his cheek.

"There ain't a thing to do, Louise," one of the fathers said from the crowd. "No way we can find out who done it, and ain't a one of us about to go poking around Nicholtown looking for one nigger that hit a white boy with a rock."

It turned out that Cal wasn't as bad off as he looked. One of the mothers in the stands, who was a nurse, said that it would probably only take a dozen or so stitches and wouldn't leave much of a scar.

Cal's momma kept screaming, and our coach couldn't decide if he should bring Cal and leave Louise in the base path, or if he should try to carry them both. From where I stood, they looked like a family that couldn't make up its mind. One of the mothers walked over and grabbed Louise under her arms. "Now, now. It's over. Let's take Cal to the doctor and get him sewed up, OK?"

Louise screamed. "I want to know who did it! Don't you want to know?" She stuck her head up and watched the crowd.

Some folks nodded their heads and some couldn't care less. Some just wanted to go home. It was no big deal to me. I'd seen that guy before. Twice. I knew all I wanted to know about him.

THE FIRST TIME I saw him was in broad daylight at the baseball field. I always came early to the field, got the key to the equipment shed from A.J., and marked off the foul lines. It was really A.J.'s job to line off the field and cut the grass and hand out ping pong paddles at the Youth Center, but he spent every afternoon on his stool in the back door of the building, drinking bottles of warm beer, looking down the hill at the baseball games. He conned some of us into doing his work for him. "It's development," he told us. "I'm letting you develop valuable skills."

By that summer, I was so developed I could lay down a straight chalk line without having to stretch a string to guide me. I'd get the key from him, open the shed near the snack bar, take out a bag of lime and the rusty push machine. Then, I'd mark off the difference between fair and foul. It was an easy thing to do if you focused your eyes on something way up ahead. If you were at home plate, you needed to look out to the corner of the outfield. Then you walked slow. But if you kept your eyes on your feet and watched the lime trickle out of the machine, you would wander all over the base path.

The afternoon I saw the black boy, I was almost to the outfield grass, dropping the trail of lime behind me, when I smelled something. It was different. It wasn't the lime dust or the railroad ties or the mowed wild onions. It was cigarette smoke, which isn't all that strange. But it's not something you expect on a little league baseball field. I turned around, and between me and home plate, the big black boy was smiling at me, dragging one of his bare feet in the dirt, erasing my line. The butt of a cigarette dangled from his huge grin. He wore a pair of blue jean shorts split way up his legs and no shirt. It looked like he had rubbed some of the new lime on his chest. I could see two white hand prints smeared across his belly.

I took off after him, but before I could make up any distance, he had already jumped the fence near the dugout and started up the hill to the tracks. When he reached the top, he didn't look back. Just leaped out of sight like a man going off a cliff. Except he was laughing.

I redid the part of the line he erased, and that evening during the game I could still smell his cigarette smoke hanging like a cloud in the thick air over the field. There were no trains that night, so no rocks, but I could feel all of those black boys, feel them watching us play our game, somehow blowing their smoke over the rails and into our field inning after inning.

When the game was over, I remembered I still had A.J.'s key tucked in my sock. I took it back and found him in the back door of the Center, staring down at the baseball field. "Don't forget to turn off the lights," I told him. There were times when he fell asleep drunk in the Center and the lights buzzed and burned all night, driving the moths crazy until daylight.

"I won't," he said. Then, "What would you have done?"

"What?"

"What would you'd done if you'da caught that big nigger today?"

The cigarette smoke filled my nose again, and I glanced over my shoulder just to make sure we were alone. All I saw was the glow from the field. "I guess I didn't think about it," I said.

A.J. took a pull from his bottle of beer. "You need to. You catch him, what you gonna do with him?" He finished the bottle and slung it toward the lights.

Sometimes, I can see what's going to happen. Tomorrow or maybe the next day, someone would run over that bottle with a lawnmower, and the day after that someone else would cut his foot on the glass.

I SAW HIM again, a few days after he erased the foul line. It was in the woods near my house. I spent a lot of time there, high up in the sycamores and oaks, smoking reeds, the kind that stuck up through the dead leaves on the ground—about as big around as a pencil, and hollow, like a straw. Once they died and turned brown, you could break them into little cigarette-size pieces, light up the end, blow out the flame and puff it while it glowed. I always headed for the trees where nobody from the neighborhood would think to look, and if it was humid enough in the woods, you could shoot out a gray cloud of smoke that settled into the limbs of the hardwoods like a fog.

One afternoon, I left the house with a book of matches, and a hundred feet into the woods, I had gathered enough reeds for an hour of smoke. For some reason, I didn't climb a tree. Instead, I just went deep enough into the woods to feel safe and sat at the base of a huge oak. I lit up, closed my eyes while the smoke swirled over my teeth, and I heard somebody laugh.

I jumped up before I opened my eyes, but when I did, he was there, maybe twenty yards in front of me. Big and sweating, he seemed comfortable with the heat in the woods. I choked on the smoke, the thick reed smoke that I never usually swallowed now deep inside my lungs. He laughed once more, then reached in his pocket. Out came an old brass lighter and a pack of Camels. He lit one up, blew the smoke out of his nose and walked through the trees toward the tracks.

I STARTED HAVING dreams where the two of us met again in the woods. He carried a baseball with him, an old one that was scuffed and yellow with age, and he showed me the autographs on the cover. Black ballplayers who had signed just their first names with a pencil in a grade-school style print. I told him I'd never heard of these players, and he laughed at me behind a fresh Camel. He had a glove, too. An old one not much bigger than a mitten. I smelled mildew and saddle soap. I followed him to an open spot in the woods and found a pitcher's mound made of Spanish moss and, sixty feet away, a wide pine stump for a catcher to sit on. There was a straight stripe of chalk line that ran from the mound to the stump. He told me this was where he practiced.

But we're on my side of the tracks, I said.

He laughed again and said that those tracks weren't nothing but a couple pieces of steel on a hill, and he and some of his friends took turns with a shovel and dug a big tunnel underneath the tracks so they could come over here and throw the baseball in the trees. I started to tell him about how I climbed the trees here and smoked reeds.

The black boy stopped me and said, *I don't wanna hear no*

shit about you and your trees. You ain't nothing to me.

He kicked at the lime with his bare foot, then he climbed the moss mound and wound up, the same slow windup I saw that evening on the tracks above our baseball field. He pushed forward and let fly, and the ball rocketed through the trees, through the center of the thick trunks. The trees bent from the force of the pitch, like saplings in a hurricane. And if you walked behind him and looked over his shoulder, you could see a straight line of holes, all the size of a baseball, and the holes seemed to go for miles and miles, until they disappeared into a single dot of darkness.

WE WERE ALL playing kick the can after dark. That's what we told our parents. The only reason they ever let us leave the house after dark was that we told them we would be playing at Kathleen Welch's house. Kathleen's daddy was the minister at First Presbyterian, and most of our parents thought that his connection with God would protect us once the sun went down. What they didn't know was that Reverend Welch slept in front of the television, and we pretty much had free run of the huge back yard. Kathleen's house was a few blocks on the other side of the Youth Center, so it was a long ride on my bike, but the dogs that always chased me couldn't see me coming in the dark, and there weren't any hills. Just a straight shot down 2nd Avenue, parallel to the tracks, then coast into Kathleen's yard.

Cal was there with his bandage on. It had been maybe a week or so since the thing with the rock. He hadn't been back to the baseball field, but it was so close to the end of the season, his mother was making him sit out until next year, when everything would be healed up. He was just supposed to watch and not sweat on his stitches. What he really did was wander through the yard in the middle of our game, while everyone else tried to stay hidden behind the hedges. He talked and gave away all of the hiding spots. He was just mad that he couldn't run or do anything. He was mad about the blood and the thin scar he was going to have. He was mad that his momma screamed and crawled around the infield on her hands and knees in front of a crowd.

Somebody said we should have a séance since we couldn't play kick the can. Kathleen ran inside her house and took a piece of candle and some matches from the kitchen drawer. She dripped a pile of wax in the grass, stood the candle up straight, and we sat in a circle around the flame. We'd have to hold hands eventually, so everyone jockeyed for positions. I ended up with Kathleen on one side of me and Cal on the other. Then, we tried to decide who we wanted to call back from the dead. We went through the usual list for this kind of thing: Kennedy, George Washington, Marilyn Monroe, crazy relatives, rich relatives. Kathleen pushed hard for Marilyn. She said she was mysterious and tragic.

"Hitler," Cal said, almost in a whisper.

"What?" I said.

"Hitler, Adolph Hitler. We need to talk to Hitler," he told us.

Kathleen said, "What you want with Adolph Hitler?"

Cal stood up. "Look at this shit," he said, pointing at his cheek. I didn't look up, but I knew what he meant. "I got this and I can't do nothing about it. If I could get Hitler here, I'd tell him everything."

"And then what?"

"Hitler wouldn't let no nigger get away with this. Everybody else might, but ain't no way Adolph Hitler'd let us get rocks chunked at us every time a train comes by," Cal said. I turned toward him. With just the little flicker of light from the candle, I could see how shiny his face was. He looked like he was going to sweat right through his stitches. "Hitler'd go over to Nicholtown and kick some butt," he said.

I wanted to laugh. No matter how mad people got, they still called it Nicholtown. Nobody ever said Niggertown even though everybody knew that's what it meant. Instead of laughing, I said, "I think it might be a little hard calling Hitler back."

From the shadows on the other side of the circle: "My daddy says he ain't really dead."

"I don't care." Cal was breathing hard now. He was walking around the circle, having some trouble talking. "I want them people over there taken care of. He stabbed his finger toward the tracks. "Line them up and take care of them."

By then, some of the other kids were beginning to like the idea of having Hitler back in the land of the living. Hitler was no Marilyn Monroe. He was no mystery. Everyone knew exactly who he was. We'd heard the stories of Hitler, how he bombed or shot or burned down the things he didn't particularly like. He would have no trouble destroying Nicholtown, turning it into a pile of ash and hot tin. Cal would probably show him the quickest way across the tracks. Once they got there, I knew they would be able to find the black boy, and I imagined what would happen when he came face to face with Hitler. I stared at the candle in the circle and wondered if he would laugh and blow smoke at Hitler's head.

I don't want to hear no shit about you, the black boy might tell Hitler. You ain't nothing to me.

I said to Cal, "You know these things ain't for real. Hitler ain't coming back."

"I aim to get me this nigger," he whispered.

"Just because you're too slow to get out of the way of a rock ain't no reason to send some ghost of Hitler across the tracks," I said under my breath.

Cal came around the circle at me. "Slow's got nothing to do with it. You afraid what might happen if I get Hitler back here? You a nigger lover or something?"

Before I could say anything, Cal spit on me. I saw it coming from up above me, like a tiny, gray bullet in the candle light. But I couldn't dodge it. It hit me softly below the eye.

"See?" he said, wiping his mouth carefully so he wouldn't disturb his stitches. "Slow has got nothing to do with it." He ran toward the street, in the direction of his house.

For a couple of minutes no one said a word. They all watched me clean my face with my t-shirt. Kathleen finally said, "I'd just as soon not have Hitler in the back yard anyway. Besides, if he isn't really dead, we'd just be wasting our time. We know Marilyn Monroe's dead as a doornail, so why don't we call her back?"

Kathleen tried her best to make Marilyn appear. She talked up to the sky. I was listening hard, trying to hear if Cal was really gone. A breeze blew out the candle and Kathleen dug her fingers into my palm. But Marilyn never showed. Reverend Welch came to the screen door and yelled at us. Told us all to go home and say our prayers.

I PEDALED FOR home, keeping an eye out for dogs that might run from the ditches. And for Cal, too. I thought he might be worked up enough to try something, even though he'd already spit on me. A block from the Youth Center, I noticed the glow, a dirty layer of gold that spread out in the air above the trees. A.J. had left the lights on again.

I propped my bike at the front of the Center. It was dark inside the building, but I'd been there enough to know where all the ping pong tables were. I weaved toward the back door and there sat A.J., leaning back a little on his stool, several empty beer bottles scattered at his feet. He was gazing off in the direction of the field. He tipped a bottle to his mouth.

He didn't turn when I walked up and stood beside his stool. He just kept staring at the field and said, "He showed up. Outta nowhere. Showed up and started."

I looked down the slope. The black boy was there, under the lights. He was running the bases with his shirt off. He was barefooted. He was playing his own game. He would stand in the batter's box, check his stance, and swing at an imaginary pitch. Then he would head for first base, round the bag, and try to stretch it into a double. I saw him slide, hooking his shin perfectly on second base.

I could barely hear his feet padding on the infield. The sound coming so late after the sight made me think that this wasn't really happening. The black boy was all of the batters, the whole team. Sometimes he struck out. Once, he hit an imaginary home run and rounded the bases in a slow trot. He waved to the crowd. He waved to the tracks. I think he even waved at us.

THE AC

THE LONG SUMMER I DABBLED IN RELIGIOUS ECSTASY,
Eddie Baxley's 1972 gray Lincoln Continental was the only
thing in our neighborhood with decent air conditioning. This
was the big, heavy model with suicide doors, the ones hinged
toward the middle of the car, in the wrong place, it seemed to
me. Once the weather went full-on hot in mid-June, my father
spent most of his afternoons in the Lincoln. He'd fill an empty
spackling bucket with Old Milwaukee cans and ice chips and
march (a military pace with as much good posture as he could
muscle) across the street to Eddie's yard, where the Lincoln sat
large and looming on the little rise above the sidewalk. Eddie
Baxley owned a garage for years and years, so he'd run across
good deals on nice cars every month or so. The Lincoln he got
for a steal. An old lady from Andrews let it run empty of oil and
the engine seized just off Highway 527. She told Eddie she'd
had enough of big, ugly cars and he could have the Lincoln for
five hundred dollars. Eddie died six months after he got the

Lincoln running again. Between Christmas and New Year's, a heart attack hit him while he lay on his mechanics creeper beneath a Ford pickup with a bad transaxle. My father slid him out by his bare white ankles and said he'd never seen a more surprised look on a dead man's face, like he'd discovered something important, like a new country.

I've never known whose idea it was to park the Lincoln in Eddie's yard and sit in the waves of cold air and watch the neighborhood shimmer in the heat on the other side of the windshield. But it sounds like something my father would've dreamed up. He was a smart man, smart enough to never put decent skin in any game he happened to play. Which is why I can see him talking Eunice Baxley into making the Lincoln the coldest place on our street and letting him set up shop with his bucket of beer. But it might've been her idea. She had been a stranger to the outside world since her husband died under the Ford. Maybe she arrived at the point that she just wanted someone to talk to. Because as far as we could tell, that's what my father and Eunice did in the front seat of the Lincoln—talk away the afternoons while the cool air blew on them.

They kept the windows cracked so they wouldn't die. And they didn't have to worry about wasting gas because they got all they needed for free, from McGill's Esso station out on Highway 52. The entire town knew Mr. McGill had family money and ran the Esso station for fun. At least that's what my old man said. Mr. McGill sipped Old Crow and Sprite from a coffee mug most of the day, so when it came time to close down the station and turn off the lights, he could never seem to remember to shut off the pumps. He would walk away and leave things running all night. My old man would sneak over to the Esso station long after dark and fill the big tank on the Lincoln. He wasn't the only one. A dozen or so people in town knew that McGill was too buzzed to shut down his pumps at closing time, and they helped themselves to some fuel as well. Everybody said McGill could spare a little, with all he had. I have come to understand now that these people saw the free gasoline as reparations for a long-since-gone offense of some nature. It was an easy, innocent revenge.

When I had twenty-five cents I felt I could part with, I sat in the back seat of the Lincoln and listened to my dad and Eunice talk. It reminded me of a kind of church. They talked in low tones, in that adult code that I had only begun to decipher. I thought if I sat there long enough, the words would start to mean something important, something I hadn't learned to figure out by myself. My mother had dragged me with her to the Kingstree Methodist Church every Sunday morning for as long as I could remember. The words there were different, all wrapped up in stained glass and candle wax and little bread cubes on a tray. There, I listened to Reverend Scoggins talk about God and the Devil and the existence of miracles in the real world. And when I had a quarter in my pocket, I listened to Eunice Baxley rant about the weather her husband tolerated in Korea and to my dad go on about Vietnam and tiny men in black pajamas. I remember thinking at the time that the Lincoln would probably do a better job than Reverend Scoggins of getting me to heaven, as long as there was enough free gas at McGill's Esso to make the trip. This was the summer religion started to confuse me.

My mother wasn't pleased about the admission fee to the Lincoln. "I can't believe you charge your own son to sit in that car," she said one evening, without looking at him. She rarely made eye contact when they discussed each other's shortcomings. I imagined she thought his eyes possessed some sort of magical x-ray power, and if she stared into them for too long, she would lose bodily functions. Granted, his eyes were strange and growing more different each day—darker and sunk deeper in his head. By the summer of the Lincoln, he was rail thin from his relentless stomach problems, and the eyes seemed to burrow backwards little by little while the rest of him retreated to the surface of his bones.

"I'm teaching these youngsters a life lesson," he said. "You want to be comfortable, you need to check the price tag. If you want a little cool air across your neck, you got to pay for that pleasure. Pleasure costs." He paused. "The cold air is a metaphor, you see."

"Maybe you can save up all those quarters you're taking from the neighborhood and buy us an air conditioner. This fan won't be much pleasure come August," she said back, and she was right. The house was hot all the time now, and the little fans my mother planted in the rooms hummed day and night, doing nothing more than stir up the hot air. The noise from all of them running and oscillating made our house sound like the world's largest active beehive. I learned to sleep without moving a muscle, which I thought was somehow cooler in the midst of the swelter. I taught myself to sleep inside the noise.

But my father wasn't saving the money. He used the quarters to buy more Old Milwaukees at the IGA food store. Sometimes the line to get into the Lincoln would be a half dozen kids long. Never any adults, always kids. We each bought a half hour for twenty-five cents, and my dad would only let two at a time into the big back seat, because, he said, he "wanted us to have enough room to stretch out and really enjoy the cold." I received special treatment because I was his son. I was allowed to go solo in the back seat. And sometimes he would let me stay more than a half hour. The inside of the Lincoln smelled like beer and pine trees. I liked to shut my eyes and feel the air moving across my skin and pretend I was at the North Pole. I listened without looking, imagining the words blowing in the air.

"You realize Eddie would tell us this isn't really cold here in this car," Eunice Baxley said. "You don't know cold, he would tell us, until you are sitting waist deep in a mud hole that's got ice floating on top of it and wondering if your toes are still attached to your feet and wondering if those infidel Chinese are going to run over the hill at you, but then you get to thinking that they are cold too because for all the things Chinamen *ain't* got, they do have toes and their boots ain't no better than yours and so Eddie figured their toes are freezing off so there will be no running involved with what they had heard was the impending invasion of mud holes by said Chinamen. That's what he'd say. If he were here." When Eunice became a spokesman for her deceased husband, she tried to spill out everything in one thin, desperate breath, like she wasn't sure she'd be allowed the chance to draw another. I supposed that's the way you begin to think when your husband rolls underneath a Ford one afternoon and never comes back.

My father always sounded more thoughtful, more philosophical when he talked about his war. "I saw a bug melt one day," he said. "This bug was pretty as it could be, all multi-colored, and it flew through the air and alighted on my gun barrel. And when he landed, he just started smoking. Little puff of smoke. Then he melted into a greasy dot of Vietnam bug goo right on the barrel." He paused. "That's how hot it was. When you can melt bugs on your gun barrel, you got some heat going, sister. Trust me on that one." He liked to let his words hang in the cold air, hovering above the low-throated idle of the big Lincoln.

There would be a silence, as they let their stories settle into the floorboards—the only sound the whirr of the air conditioner. I felt the Lincoln rumbling under me. And Eunice would inevitably reach across from her passenger's seat and touch my father's hand. "Eddie, Eddie, dammit," she said, and I swear they forgot anybody else was in the air conditioning, as rapt as they were by the strength of their sad recollections.

The hotter the summer became, the more time Eunice and my father spent in the air conditioning. On Sunday mornings, my mother would half-heartedly ask my father if he was going to put in an appearance at church, and he would say, "Well, as a matter of fact, I'm heading to my place of worship right now." Then he hauled the spackling bucket across the street to the Lincoln. We'd leave him there and drive our own car to the Methodist Church. "I don't worry about him ending up in hell," my mother said one morning on the way to church. "He'd figure out some way to make it fun. Or make a profit."

I asked her once if it bothered her that Dad sat in a car most of the day with a woman. She said of all the things that bothered her about my father, him perched in hot broad daylight with a woman who couldn't figure out how to let go of the dead was low on the list. "You don't have to keep an eye on sad people much," she said with the air of someone handing down a commandment. "Sad isn't dangerous."

At church, I liked to watch Reverend Scoggins from the second or third pew. Before he began every sermon, he made a big production of pulling his handkerchief from a hidden pocket in his black cassock. He snapped the starched folds out of it and put the cloth to his mouth, like a man wiping away a dab of barbeque sauce. Once he'd cleaned his lips, he closed his eyes and in a sawmill whisper that even the back pew could hear, he'd say, "Let the words of my mouth and the meditations of our hearts be acceptable in thy sight, oh Lord, our strength and our redeemer." Then, he gave a slight glance toward heaven or the ceiling and started his sermons. I only understood the most general gist of what he spoke about. Usually about living the right way when you can and asking for forgiveness when you don't. I realized then I was destined to spend a lot more time in my life looking to be forgiven than doing the right things, which wasn't so much a depressing thought as it was exhausting. I foresaw myself as a man chasing around somebody or something that would give me a pass for my indiscretions, both purposeful and accidental. But that summer, I had no clue what a decent indiscretion was.

Truth be told, I was addled. I had begun to spend my nights lying in the dark, blanketed by only the hot air, worrying about the nature of heaven, what it looked like, what kind of places folks lived in. Whether they would allow people to sit in air conditioned cars and swap stories. Were there even cars in heaven, for that matter? From what I could tell from Reverend Scoggins, gold was a prominent feature in the afterlife unless you went straight to Hell, which made me wonder if the fact that we did not have an air conditioner was simply a rehearsal for the future, preparing ourselves for the sizzle of eternal flames. Admittedly, I had too much time on my hands that summer, and I wasn't sure if my friends were concerned with their afterlives, because I never asked them. Me and Lonnie Tisdale and the McElveen brothers talked about girls we'd considered kissing and the size of redbreasts we'd hooked in the Black River, but never once did I ask them about the nature of their souls. It wasn't the kind of thing that came up by itself.

I did ask my mother. I told her that church made me nervous.

"What do you mean nervous? Does your stomach hurt? Do you make sure you go to the bathroom before services?" she asked. Although she was a nurse and well-practiced in professional and amateur diagnoses, she was convinced every ailment with her children originated with the lack of regular bowel movement.

"It's more like I can't sleep and I spend all my time worrying about things after I get back from church," I said. "Things like hell."

She glanced out the window across the street, toward the Lincoln. "Like you could tell me anything about worry," she said. I knew what she meant. No matter how much she insisted Eunice Baxley was harmless, she still wondered what went on in the Lincoln. She'd asked me about it one afternoon, and I told her that Eunice and my dad just talked about wars and dead people. That was it. I didn't tell her about Eunice's wandering hand. I could tell she wasn't convinced. She was over feeling sorry for my father, for his half a stomach and the way he kept shrinking into himself. He'd run out of excuses for his own weaknesses, so these days, she was content to let events drift by, like leaves on the surface of Black River.

"And I worry about dying and everything," I said trying to pull the conversation back toward me.

"Get used to it," she said, fanning herself with a dishtowel. For a nurse, she could be pretty harsh inside her own house. "Listen, I got enough worrying all to myself. That's what church is for. Church is where you go to clear your head. So you just keep sitting there beside me and listen to Scoggins and one day a switch will flip on and you'll get about half of life figured out. The other half will stay a mystery. Half is about the best you can hope for." She mopped her face with the towel. "Go see if that fan is turned up all the way, would you? It's hot as hell in here."

She smiled when she said that. She knew what she was doing. That night, it was all I could do not to think about burning up eternally.

The next day was Sunday, which makes sense now—that I would spend a night tossing and turning, then drive off to church, fuzzy-headed and anxious again. Reverend Scoggins performed his little handkerchief drama, then preached about King David and Bathsheba. I tried to do what my mother suggested, let a switch flip, let half of the world come clear in my head, but it didn't seem to be happening. Scoggins appeared to enjoy reciting the story of a king's fall from grace. He had the same expression on his face people in town flashed when they bragged about stealing gas from McGill's Esso station—a guilt-free smile that oozed satisfaction. Scoggins' face glowed down to us, and I watched my mother fighting to stay awake. I wondered if she'd had trouble sleeping too.

I do recall at one point, David attempts to convince Bathsheba's husband to come back from the war and lay with his wife. (My mother glanced toward me when Scoggins said "lay with," and I nodded up at her because my friends and I had already discussed the cryptic words in the Bible, a language not unlike the adult code we'd begun to crack. She knew I knew.)

David, from where I sat, kept digging himself a deeper and deeper hole, and God watched every shovelful. My head bobbed and bobbed. I did my best to fight sleep, to listen to Scoggins' words, but they turned into a lullaby somehow, and right when the reverend got to the part where David asked for forgiveness, I couldn't keep my head on my shoulders, and the last thing I remember was a blast of gold light that flashed across my eyes when I fell sideways and cracked my forehead square on the pew.

IN HER FLAT nurse's monotone, my mother said I bled relatively little for such a big split on my head. "I've seen worse," she said. "Your skin is very thin there, you know." My mother didn't realize that toppling over in the pew—and interrupting church for a half hour while they carried me out and wiped up the blood—had scrambled the thoughts flitting around my head. I'd heard about religious ecstasy. I looked it up in the library. And I knew from my research that most people were wide awake when they had their strange, religious spells. I'd been out cold. But while I was out, David and Bathsheba and Eunice and my old man and Eddie Baxley and God and my mother jumbled together. Everyone's story became my *single* story, buzzing in my head like a pissed off bee in a jar. My mother told me the first thing I said when I floated toward consciousness was: "What did God do to daddy when he came back from the war to lay with Bathsheba? Did King David make it back from Korea?"

She said Reverend Scoggins stood above me, and the two of them chalked my nonsense up to a nasty, enlarging bump on the head, at least until I looked at Scoggins clear-eyed and said, "Does everybody get forgiven in the end?" She told me when I said that to him, the blood drained from his face a little, like he'd been asked a question he couldn't answer. "Boy needs some rest," he said, and he went back to the pulpit to finish off David and Bathsheba.

I wobbled some when I walked, propped against my mother's side all the way to the car, and she opened the windows so I could get as much air as possible on the ride home. My forehead was wrapped in a piece of purple cloth that felt silky to the touch and smelled slightly of stale cologne. I'm not sure when she made her plan, but my mother didn't turn right into our driveway, instead went left and pulled across the grass and up the slope and threw the car in park, right beside the Lincoln.

My father lowered the driver's window and looked through the slice of space. "How was church?" he asked.

"Your son had a moment," she said. "Open that back door for me. It's too damn hot in the house for him right now." She helped me out of the car. "And if you say anything about needing a quarter, I'll beat you senseless." My father jumped out of the Lincoln, flustered as if he suddenly had houseguests he hadn't prepared for. She gave me a slight nudge into the back seat, and it felt like it always did, like ducking into a big walk-in cooler. My hand made its way instinctively toward my pocket to search for a quarter that wasn't there.

"Hello, Eunice," my mother said, her voice caked with sugary sarcasm. "I hope you're having yet another productive day on earth." To me, she said, "When you feel better, walk on home. We're the house right across the street. The one you can see *real good* from the front seat of this damn car." I waited for her to slam the door, but she held back and just eased it shut, like a quiet taunt.

For a solid minute or so, the silence blew around us until I decided Eunice and my old man were waiting for me to open the discussions. "I passed out in church," I said.

"What's that ribbon on your head?" my father asked.

"That thing the preacher drapes around his neck sometimes," I said back. "They needed a bandage. I was bleeding for a while."

Eunice spoke, her voice more ragged than usual. "How you feeling now?" She didn't turn in her seat, just continued to stare out the window. Before I could answer, she said, "Why there goes Laurice Reeves on her bicycle. She doesn't look like she went to church."

I didn't know how she could tell at this distance that somebody had not attended services. "I'm okay, I guess," I said, feeling a little neglected. To be honest, I hadn't taken inventory of my faculties. My head didn't hurt all that much, not more than a little throb every now and then behind my eyes. I couldn't explain it (and I can't to this day), but I felt different somehow, like a bang on the head had shaken something loose. I felt as though the person I was *before* church was a little bit of a stranger this afternoon. I wondered if this was what my mother meant when she told me changes were coming. I didn't realize they would come this fast. Or that I'd have to smack my head on a church pew to bring them about. But something had indeed changed.

"Me and Eunice were just talking about the rise of communism," my father said.

"Bullshit," I told him. He snapped his head around.

"What did you say?" he hissed, then glanced at Eunice to see if she'd heard.

The purple bandage on my head draped one of my eyes and I tugged it up so I could look straight at him. "I said that's all bullshit. You aren't talking about communism. You're just talking about anything so you can sit in the cold with somebody who will at least listen to you." I pulled at the bandage again. "I speak the truth, Father."

He stared at me like he was studying a map of land he'd never set foot in. "I think you better mind that tongue of yours."

The end of the purple bandage hung off the side of my head, long enough that I could grab the end of it and dab at my mouth, which I did, and quickly followed with, "Let the words of my mouth and the meditations of our hearts be acceptable in thy sight, Daddy."

"We aren't doing anything wrong here," Eunice said. "Your father is just helping me get beyond Eddie."

I'll bet I'd never said more than fifty words to Eunice Baxley until that afternoon, when I told her Eddie was happy where he was, happier than he'd ever been before. She winced at that. "I think you ought to cut your ties with Eddie and live out your earthly days in peace," I said.

I should confess, I had no idea where my vocabulary was coming from. It was like a typewriter in my head was spitting out sentences through my mouth. I was surprised at what I was saying and who I was saying it to, but I liked it. It felt good, like the air conditioning.

"Your mother put you up to this," my dad said. He opened his door. "I'll set her straight." He started to ease out into the brightness.

"She worries about you, you know," I told him, and that stopped him in his tracks, which I knew was going to happen. I remember smiling at the realization I could tell the future to an extent.

"What are you talking about?" The door was still open and the cold air fought with the outside heat, and it was losing the battle.

"She worries about your stomach and how it seems to be getting worse. She worries about you spending all your time in a Lincoln with another woman. She worries about money. She worries about me and Eli and what's going to happen to all of us. She spends a lot of time sitting in the living room worrying." I folded my hands and laid them in my lap.

Eunice spoke up first. "Like I said, we weren't doing anything. I'm too old for your father anyway."

"Be quiet, Eunice," my father said, then looked at me. "And you don't know what the hell you're talking about. You're just a kid. Act like one." His eyes came back then. They weren't as dark and buried in their sockets. I don't know if it was the way the bright light from the sunlight hit them, but I saw them clearly for the first time in what seemed like years. And I could see that he was afraid in his eyes, not afraid of me, but afraid of things changing. That's why he liked Eunice and the Lincoln. It was the same thing every time, every day on the hill during the hot part of the day. He could depend on that, on something staying the same. And he could hide from everything else that shimmered in the heat on the other side of the windshield.

"I'm going back to the house," I said and climbed out of the car. I adjusted the bandage on my head. The place where my forehead split was beginning to throb with a little more desperation. My father didn't move. Eunice reached over and cranked up the fan on the AC a little.

"You need to stay away from church," my father said. I stuck my hands in my pockets and shrugged my shoulders. I felt the edges of a quarter I didn't know I had. It had appeared like some kind of summer miracle. I didn't hand it to my father. I tossed it toward his open window, and he fumbled with the catch. The quarter disappeared into tall grass that needed cutting. "I'm going home," I said. "'Bye, Eunice."

I walked all the way to McGill's with my bandage wrapped around my forehead, like I was marching home wounded from war. The Esso station was between my house and the river, downhill most of the way. When I started out, I thought I would be a little light-headed, because of the heat and the throbbing across my forehead, but the closer I got to the station, the better I felt about things.

Emerson McGill liked to open his station right after church for people who wanted to fill their tanks for the upcoming week. He probably figured he could pump enough gas and sell enough Pepsi to make it worth his while. I stayed on the sidewalk the whole time while I walked, looking forward for cracks in the cement. I don't remember seeing another person the whole trip.

The front door of the station was wide open. Mr. McGill sat behind a glass counter of candy and cigarettes, fanning himself with a bulletin from the Baptist Church. I could see the line drawing of the big church building passing back and forth in front of his face. In the open back door, he'd propped

51

a huge warehouse fan that sucked air from behind the station and blew it into the tiny office space. On the wall, clipboards stuffed with orders and invoices fluttered like wind chimes. "You got a sash on your head, son," Mr. McGill said.

"I had an accident in church," I said. His coffee mug sat close by his free hand. He stopped fanning and took a sip.

"Ain't we all," he said.

I didn't know how to answer that, so I launched into my proposition. I asked Mr. McGill if he'd noticed that he was missing a lot more gas than he was selling.

"Well, my numbers don't always jive," he said, waving at the clipboards, "but I was never good at arithmetic. I figured something was wrong with the pumps."

I told him that I wasn't going to name names because that wouldn't be the Christian thing to do. (I believe I might have made that up. I am not sure that turning in thieves is *precisely* the Christian thing to do.) But I said that I could solve his mathematics-and-pump dilemma for the low, low price of five dollars a week.

He sipped again. "Let me get this straight. I'll pay you five bucks every week and give you the keys to the pumps, just so you can make sure they's turned off," he said, "and I'm going to make money with this operation?"

"You're giving away more than five dollars' worth of gas every week," I said. "I mean, do the math, Mr. McGill." That might have been mean, but I was reaching for a dramatic effect.

He took a longer sip from his coffee mug and reached underneath the candy display. He pulled out a leather wallet the size of a paperback book and fished a five dollar bill from among the slips of scrap paper and receipts.

"Here. It's worth a five to see if you're a con man or a genius." He slid the bill to me, then dug through a drawer in the cash register for the pump keys. They didn't really look like keys to me. He walked me outside and showed me how they worked. "It never occurred to me that people would actually steal gasoline," he said, shaking his head. "People aren't right in the head sometimes." Later that same afternoon, I rode my bicycle down the easy hill toward the river to the Esso station and clicked off the pumps just before the evening settled in. I made money that summer.

The Lincoln ran out of gas sometime in July. I'd like to say it was around Independence Day, but that would more than likely be a lie. I watched my father ease the car off the hill toward the gas station one night, and I knew he wouldn't be able to pump any fuel into the tank. He pulled the car back into its customary spot a few minutes later, and the next day, he and Eunice abandoned their daily rituals when the engine idled for the last time. I knew he was too cheap and broke to pay for his comfort, and Eunice was too mixed up by grief to understand why the Lincoln's engine was suddenly dead. In two weeks, the grass and weeds crept up the tires and from my house you could see the brown summer dust layering the windshield of Eddie Baxley's Lincoln.

My father started spending his days on our back porch, chasing a square of shade that ran during the day from west to east. I'm not sure if my mother was happy about him being around, but I did hear the two of them talking more. I ended up with a little scar that runs diagonal across my forehead. Not exactly stigmata, but I do find myself touching it each time I walk inside a church.

MAY MACINTOSH FLIES, JOHN WAYNE RUNS

WHEN MAY MCINTOSH KISSED ME ON THE TRAMPOLINE, I never considered the fact that I might lose my balance. I was in the seventh grade and she was a tenth grader at the private school in town, but I was tall for my age. I might have fooled her in the half-light of the evening. May must have been drinking something that night because her mouth tasted of coconuts. At the time, I had never been kissed by a girl that particular way, so for all I knew, every woman in the known world possessed a mouth tropical and exotic.

My mistake was immediately believing that a kiss from a tenth grader, with the whorl of coconut in my mouth and nose, was an invitation to other unexplored locales. Hence, the rushed attempt to slide my hand under the soft, thin cheerleading sweater May wore was met with a traditional elbow block and a laugh. "Really now," she said and it was not a question, and that was the first moment I'd ever felt stunned and rejected in front of a pretty girl, the first toppled domino in what has been a long, winding parade of less-than-edifying encounters with women with wonderful tasting mouths.

But on that night when I was thirteen, I buzzed from the hint of coconut on my tongue and even rejection seemed like a foreign country that might be nice to visit. May gave me a little peck on the lips to let me know that all was forgiven. "You're so cute," she said and fell back on the trampoline, bouncing the two of us into the air. We were at Teddy Gordan's birthday party. Teddy and I had been friends since the first grade. I was there because Teddy's parents were wealthy and always threw good parties for their children and owned a trampoline. May was there because Teddy's sister was a cheerleader and a car carrying the entire squad pulled up after Teddy cut his cake, a car full of loud, overly enthusiastic girls, some of whom had recently discovered the joys of Coco Lopez.

May was on the small cheerleading squad because she was tiny, and consequently the girl most often tossed in the air and caught by two of the larger cheerleaders anchored to the ground. I didn't go to that private school. My father did not believe that white flight was a trend with any legs to it, and he was convinced the new school would close its doors as fast as it had opened them. "That's not a school," he'd said one evening. "It's a daycare center with a bad football team." And he had a point. The school, which was called Low Country Academy, announced that it would field a football team almost before they announced they would hold English and math classes. The school's board, which was comprised of the town's wealthiest white people who still had children of school age, saw football as a thick, brave barricade across streets that led from the other side of the railroad tracks into town, a barricade to keep the black people in their places. The board's rationale was, if they could get enough boys to come to Low Country Academy and play football, the girls would follow, as would the academic curriculum. They built a school around a solid offensive line, and in my father's opinion, this would never hold. "You wait," he said. "They won't last two seasons. I mean, years."

When the trampoline settled, May sat up and said, "You go to the public school, don't you?" I nodded, unable to articulate much at that point, what with the coconut taste settling on my teeth and the thought of how close I had come to touching an actual breast buzzing in my head. "What is it like over there?" And when she asked that question, I saw perhaps the one advantage I had being a public school kid. I was somehow, some way surviving in a dangerous land. May—and everyone like her who had barely enough sense to get out of the rain during a downpour—viewed me much the way someone sees a convict paroled from a maximum security prison. *We know things they don't… and we have lived to tell the tale.* I wondered if such knowledge could gain me safe passage beneath the L or C or A across May McIntosh's sweater.

I never had the opportunity that evening to whisper tales of public school brutality and degradation in May McIntosh's ear. The main reason is that none existed. A desegregated school had proven to be as boring as the segregated one. I had some good teachers and I had some bad. I had made some new friends, some of them black, guys who knew football and music. And I had kept most of my old friends who had fled to Low Country Academy. The other reason is, about the time I leaned toward May for more coconuts and stories, a car on the other side of the house blew its horn and she said, "That's Alissa. I have to go." She rolled backwards to her feet, some kind of trampoline-style-sitting somersault, then bounced to her feet. She clapped twice for herself which I now consider rather melodramatic, but at that moment seemed like the perfect way to categorize all of our performances. Worth applause, just not too much.

"You should come to a game sometime," she said, then disappeared around the dark corner of the house, leaving me running my tongue over my teeth, hoping for coconut.

"ALL OF THEM ran," my father said at dinner a few nights later. His most interesting commentaries on the world outside his front door occurred at dinner, after he'd had an entire afternoon of drinking Old Milwaukee and contemplating the current state of affairs. "Why do you think the newspapers— the big ones, not like the one you deliver," he said, nodding to me, "why do you think they all call it white flight? Because those people ran. John Wayne never ran." None of us seated at the table eating greasy chicken from a paper bucket needed an explanation for the John Wayne reference. For my father, John Wayne was symbolic of America, or more specifically, the way America should always conduct itself. My father's politics were a twisted network of illogical threads, yet the one thing that remained constant was his idea that if we were all like John Wayne, we would live in a world one slide-step from paradise. When my father paused, my brother and I waited in the silence for my mother's answer. She was always the person who goaded him.

Finally, she said, "John Wayne doesn't live in South Carolina. He lives in Hollywood. They don't have black people in Hollywood." She was still dressed in her nurse's uniform. She'd picked up the chicken from the Bantam Chef on her way home from the hospital. When my father closed his eyes and groaned, she winked at us. She hated the John Wayne metaphor as much as we did. Those years, there was no movie theater in town. This was our entertainment: watching our nurse mother nudge her husband right to the edge of a nervous breakdown a couple of times week.

"THAT IS NOT THE POINT," he said. "If John Wayne were here, he would not run and hide in a school that looks like a car dealership." Low Country Academy was currently occupying the space that formerly housed Longstreet Chevrolet. The history classes met in the same area where my father used to get his oil changed, and he could not recover from that tiny bit of trivia.

"I could write John Wayne a letter," my brother said. Eli was at the age where the most mysterious and wonderful relationship in the world was the pen pal. He'd spent most of the previous summer writing letters to strangers and mailing them across the country, even one to Canada. "I could ask him to come talk to us about it."

My mother reached for gravy. "I think that's a wonderful idea," she said, and my brother asked immediately if he could be excused.

"You haven't touched that breast on your plate," my father said, and I felt myself blush with the memory of the trampoline and May McIntosh's cheerleading sweater. I was a terrible blusher. My face flamed at the mere mention of anything slightly uncomfortable or embarrassing. I have never been able to play poker. "Look at him," my father said, pointing across the table at my face. "Can't even say the word breast without making him squirm. Jesus. Puberty. Pass me the gravy."

My little brother ran from the table and disappeared, not even returning for his biscuit and honey. After I cleaned all the trash from the table, he hissed from the top of the stairs and waved a piece of paper at me. Up in his room, he said, "Make sure all my spelling's correct and stuff." On a piece of Blue Horse notebook paper, he'd scrawled out a message to John Wayne. The greeting was very formal: Dearest Mr. John Wayne, Movie Star. The rest of it turned a little rugged:

> *We were eating chicken tonight and talking about you.*
> *My father says you never ran from nothing if more people*
> *were like you we wouldn't have 2 schools in town and 1*
> *of them is all full up with white people who ran. When*
> *can you come explain to us how not to run away from*
> *things like black people. We are always hear so you can*
> *come any time I like True Grit alot. Your friend, Eli*

"You're missing a question mark," I said. I decided not to mention any of the other errors. I didn't want to dent his enthusiasm. "You got an address for John Wayne?"

"It'll get there," he said. "It's Hollywood," and ran off to find my mother, who by now was in the living room, with her feet up on the couch that nobody but her ever bothered to use. My brother had not mastered the art of looking up zip codes in the big book at the post office. He depended on my mother for that.

BY THE TIME a few weeks of the new school year passed, I had figured out that I would not have to work very hard in any of my classes. The teachers that I knew or recognized from the year before had this dazed look in their eyes and it was easy to see that they had given up trying to teach a class that ran the gamut from barely literate to college-bound. And the new teachers, many of whom were black, tended to circle together and spent most of their time glancing over their shoulders for the threat they felt sure was looming nearby. The result was: we were given text books, told to read them on our own, and any tests would come from the end of the chapters. I spent most of the first few weeks reading comic books. Rusty Thomasson, who sat in front of me, decided he would read the Bible cover to cover. Most people slept on their desks. The only person I saw with a nose in a textbook was Columbus Jones, a tall, rail-thin black boy with Buddy Holly glasses and saddle oxford shoes. The glasses were too big for his face and kept slipping down his nose while he read. His fingers constantly flicked at his face, pushing the glasses back into place.

Early in the year, during one of the bathroom breaks, Columbus Jones walked up to me in front of the urinal and said, "Why you watching me so much?" He and I were about the same height, both long for our ages and growing out of the hem of our pants on a regular basis. His chin stuck out a little like he was expecting a fight. "Why don't you get some glasses that fit?" I said, and he and I were good after that, as though we simply needed to ask each other a couple of questions that remained unanswered to launch a friendship.

Looking back, Columbus and I complimented each other well. For instance, my musical tastes pretty much centered around the Monkees at that point, a fact I am to this day ashamed to admit. (In my defense, the Monkee I most admired was Michael Nesmith because he looked to be actually playing his guitar.) But Columbus filled in some gaps for me. He knew everything about Motown, and he brought his transistor radio to school to educate me on the music that spilled out of Detroit. In the back of the playground, at recess, he would pull his contraband radio from inside his corduroy pants and dial in a station I had never bothered with. He played the Supremes and the Jackson Five and Smokey Robinson and the Miracles. He would hold the radio in the air as though he were trying to attract the AM waves, and he would dance to "ABC" and imitate little Michael Jackson. The first couple of times he did this, I glanced around and tried to keep myself hidden, afraid I would be spotted by someone who cared what was going on in the back of the field. But the fact was, nobody gave a shit one way or the other. We could have been building bombs or drinking Thunderbird. Nobody cared because caring meant you had to do something about it. And I think that particular fall, everybody was through trying to fix things that were broken. I don't recall a whole lot of anger then, just a lot of airy resignation, like the world somehow let go with a giant sigh that blew over all of us.

I DIDN'T THINK about football until weather turned a bit and we finally had a frost. We didn't have many cold nights in Kingstree. We were too close to the coast for a decent winter, always seeming to gather the wind that blew fairly warm off the ocean, but there was that day, usually in October, when the grass crunched under your feet and you had to walk with your hands in your coat pockets. That was the day I decided to go to a football game at Low Country Academy and watch May McIntosh fly through the air.

I had not forgotten about her. In fact, I saw her a couple of times at Teddy Gordan's house, usually on the weekends when I was visiting, seeing how high I could get on the trampoline. She'd pull up in a car with Teddy's sister and wave as she ran in the house, her short legs churning circles across the lawn. I wondered if the coconut taste ever really left her mouth, if she carried it with her everywhere she went, like a fingerprint. I convinced myself, as I bounced in the air, that she smiled differently when she saw me—a signal, an acknowledgement of the kiss on the trampoline. It wasn't true, of course. I had, at that age, not yet learned those types of exchanges rarely existed. It takes years and years to develop the code. May McIntosh and I hadn't had enough time yet.

That first chilly afternoon, I walked into my house and asked my mother if I could go to the football game on Friday night. She was about to grant permission when my father called from his chair at the table, "Which one?" In the past, my parents had let me ride my bike to the public high school and watch from outside the fence. You could see the lights of that stadium from my front yard. Low Country Academy was a different story. The school had a brand new football field that had been plowed up on a few acres of flood plain near the river. Somebody donated the land to the school and received free tuition for life for his kids. The booster club was in charge of seeding the plot of land and keeping it mowed once the grass started growing in late August. From what I'd been told, the field wasn't all that well lit, only a pole at each corner of the end zones, and on those poles, only a couple of spotlights. To get to the game, I'd have to catch a ride with somebody or pedal several miles in the dark.

"The private school game," I said, still looking at my mother.

"Why you want to go watch those boys?" my father said. "Just a bunch of country club dove hunters who can't run in a straight line."

My mother said. "Are you going alone?"

"I hadn't really thought about it," I said. "It's only Wednesday."

My father wasn't listening to us. "They can't run a football. Only thing they know about running is getting away from black people. Hell, all the good athletes are still at the public high school. Everybody knows that."

Something clicked in my head, like a switch had been thrown. I turned to my father. "I was thinking about going with somebody from school," I said. "His name is Columbus. He's a black kid."

His eyes widened. He cocked his head slightly as if he were hearing a faint noise on a breeze nobody else in the room could feel. It was one of the few times he'd looked at me like I wasn't his son, that person always in his way, always costing him money, asking him questions he didn't want to answer. It was an expression just shy of pride.

"You want to go to a Low Country Academy football game with a black boy?" he said slowly. He shook his head and studied the can of Old Milwaukee on the table in front of him. "Well, I'll drive then. I wouldn't miss that."

MY BROTHER HAD quit checking the mail for a Hollywood postmark, so when the large envelope came from Batjac Studios, it was my mother who presented it to him. "That's where I sent your letter," she said. "That's John Wayne's company. Don't rip everything up. You'll want the envelope for a souvenir."

Eli took a kitchen knife and slid it under the flap. "Y'all don't watch. You're making me nervous," he said. "I'm going to my room." My mother put her arm out to stop me from following, so we sat there at the table until he returned.

"I don't get it," he said. He waved a photograph in front of us then let it flutter the table. It was a big picture, a black and white, of John Wayne, all decked out in cowboy gear. He sneered at the camera, something like a smile but with attitude behind it. Written in a perfect cursive across the photo was a message: *To Eli… Best wishes, The Duke.*

My mother was a nurse. She was accustomed to saying things without sugar-coating them. "Well, that's pretty standard issue," she said.

My brother turned the envelope over and shook it, hoping he'd missed something the last twenty times he'd checked the contents.

"He doesn't say anything about coming to see us. And he sure doesn't say anything about running away from black people," he said. He wasn't so much sad as he was confused.

"Honey, he was never going to come see us," my mother said. "He's way too busy. Plus, he doesn't really know about the whole running away thing. That's something your father made up. John Wayne doesn't understand the South. He's not from here." She ruffled his head.

"I guess," my brother said, "John Wayne wouldn't know how to act in Kingstree."

WHEN FRIDAY CAME, I felt bad I had not tried to get word to May McIntosh that I would be coming to see her. I felt like she would want to know. It never occurred to me that May McIntosh couldn't give two shits what I did with my Friday nights. That lesson—the one that dictated I would always be more enamored with women than they were with me—did not take hold until years in the future. On that particular Friday night of that particular fall, I was convinced that May McIntosh had been pining for a second kiss, and all of those secret, coded smiles were toothy invitations to place myself somewhere in her general vicinity on a night cold enough to require a blanket we could both gather beneath.

My father never mentioned driving me to the game again. His inability to follow through on anything was not a news flash. His life was a series of daily inspirations, each of which was quickly extinguished by a steady torrent of Old Milwaukee beer by mid-afternoon. On Friday morning, before I left for school, I thought he might say something about the game and about Columbus, but the only thing he asked was if I'd seen his spackling bucket full of fishing gear. For my father, fishing meant disappearance to god knows where. More codes, more signals I didn't understand. The one time my mother interrogated him about where he went on his extended angling adventures, he asked her how many days she'd spent in-country. When she didn't answer, he said, "Zero. Exactly. There are no redbreast in Vietnam. I'm going fishing." The only person in the family who understood his logic was him. The rest of us had learned to roll our eyes.

Columbus wasn't interested either, since his skills of self-preservation were more attuned and tested than mine. He was the more mature of the two of us. "I don't think that would be a good idea," he said, "showing up at a white football game. If the two of us got in, I'm not real sure we'd get out." And he was right. I hadn't thought ahead. That wasn't something you did in the seventh grade.

Columbus's interest changed when I told him about May McIntosh and the coconut kiss and the topography beneath her cheerleading sweater. He, it turned out, had never experienced a kiss. I told him about how May McIntosh was tossed into the air and spun like a trapeze artist and always landed in a web of arms, mere inches from the ground. "Now, that I would like to see," he said, so we made plans to meet near school on our bikes and pedal the couple of miles to the new Low Country Academy football field. I told him we didn't have to go near the stands, that we could watch from the trees on the far side of the field. We'd only be forty or fifty yards from the game and we could spy on the cheerleaders from there. But I was guessing at that point. I didn't know how far away from the action we'd be. I didn't even know how thick the trees were. I decided to act like I knew what I was talking about and improvise if and when the need arose. I remember thinking how pleased my father would be at that moment, how proud he would be of how I covered up what I didn't know with a thick jungle-canopy of bullshit.

I don't remember Columbus and me talking much on the dark ride to the football field. I do recall him reminding me how much faster he was than me, when he said that things might go south and we'd have to run for it. "They ain't catching me. But you," he said, "you're a different story." But nobody saw us skirt the back of the field on the hard-packed sand road and park our bikes out of the range of the dim lights, near the cypress trees that edged the far sideline. Nobody sat on that side of the field. Both teams occupied the opposite side. All the fans, home and visitor, huddled on the two skinny sets of aluminum bleachers.

We jogged in the shadows, keeping the glow of the lights and the noise on our right shoulder. I had not considered a couple of things. First, when they plowed the field, they had actually raised it a good bit, building a type of dirt wall between the trees and the field proper, to keep the swamp water from creeping in. This meant that you could actually lie on your belly and peek over the edge of the dirt barricade and watch the game from ground level. The other thing was: I never considered that somebody else would have this same idea, that somebody else who didn't want to be seen would pick the dark side of the field to watch the game. This second revelation came fast on the heels of the first. When Columbus and I stepped out of the trees, I could see the dirt wall and the slanted bank where we could lay. The next thing I saw was about a half dozen boys—public high school boys—smoking cigarettes and passing around a bottle and not even watching the game.

One of them, the one wearing a hunting coat with the collar turned up, saw us. "What the hell you doing here?" he said. The rest of his group turned toward us. I thought about running, but I remembered what Columbus said about me being slow.

"We just came to watch football," I said.

"We?" he said back, peering into the trees behind me. That was when I realized that Columbus had never broken into the dim light and was probably halfway back to his bike. He was already smart enough at that age to check before stepping out of shadows.

Something happened on the field, something good for the Low Country Academy because the roar was loud and local, rolling in from the stands opposite us. I peered over the edge of the dirt and saw somebody in green and white jogging into the end zone. Just up from the end zone, the cheerleaders—even those who didn't understand football—shook their pompoms, and the more athletic of them jumped and cleared the ground.

"Shit," one of the boys said. "They need to lose. They don't need to be scoring."

"There she goes," said another one. He had buzz cut hair and hadn't taken his eye off the field the whole time. Like a line of kittens following a ball, the boys turned in unison toward the field and forgot all about me. Across the field, the larger cheerleaders tossed May McIntosh into the air. I recognized her, even from a distance. She flipped once and decorated her descent with a half-twist. When she landed, two of the cheerleaders who caught her military pressed her into the air, where May McIntosh struck a pose with her arms upraised in a touchdown signal and one of her legs extended out and up. "Damn," one of the boys said and all of the others murmured and shook their heads in disbelief, as if they'd just witnessed someone make a mockery of the laws of gravitation and physics.

May McIntosh dropped to the ground and the attention turned back to me. "Why you out here?" the guy in the hunting coat, who seemed to be a leader of some kind, asked. "You're a little young for this, aren't you, fuzz nuts?" He tipped his bottle at me.

I wondered if Columbus was already on his bike, pedaling back toward the tracks. Hunting Coat stood up and I could see he was country skinny, the mean kind of thin, all bone and muscle and anger without a shred of logic. I pointed across the field. "That's May McIntosh," I said.

"Huh?" he said.

"That girl doing all the flipping. May McIntosh is her name," I said.

The boy with his eyes on the field said, "We know her name."

I don't know why I thought May McIntosh could rescue me from a distance, but I knew all my options for the next half hour weren't good ones. I was either going to get beat up or have cheap liquor poured down my throat or both. I couldn't run because I'd never get away from a whole team of them. I decided I had to use May McIntosh as a shield. "I was making out with her not too long ago," I said. "I put my hand on one of her titties." It was at that moment that I witnessed the power of the female breast. It was as if I had been hoisted high and struck a pose, and they were the ones charged with keeping me in the air. They immediately wanted to know what it felt like, what it looked like. I would've thought country boys like this, from out in Greeleyville or Lane would have years of experience with breasts, but I was wrong. They weren't as old as they looked and not as educated as I suspected. I felt like Marco Polo coming back with knowledge of a foreign land. They couldn't take their eyes off me. Cheers erupted from the football field, but nobody turned toward the dirt. Hunting Coat passed me the bottle but I turned it down with a simple raised palm and a look on my face that suggested, *No thanks, I've already had my fill tonight.* They wanted to know everything they could about May McIntosh, so I told as many lies as I could fabricate. I even told them about the coconut flavor that steeped inside her mouth and I told them about the curves that fit perfectly in my palm. The last thing I said was, "Boys, I'm all talked out. I got to go home before I lose my voice." It was something my father might say. I sounded just like him, and a shiver wormed its way down my back when I heard it.

Hunting Coat took a step toward me. "We come out here every time there's a home game. You come on back and let us know what's going on with May," he said and his team nodded behind him. Another cheer rolled toward us. "Dammit, I think they scored again. At least we'll see May do her stuff," the kid lying on the dirt said. They were suddenly friends with May McIntosh. They knew things now. They knew now what the inside of her mouth tasted like.

I waved at them and dipped into the woods, probably deeper than I needed to. I walked through ankle-deep swamp water and mud. I found my way back to my bike. Columbus' bike was still leaning against a tree next to mine. I immediately ran through what could have happened. He could be lost in the swamp somewhere, wandering among trees that looked the same in every direction. But that didn't make sense with the glow from the field always there as a landmark. He could've fallen down and got knocked out. I wondered if there was another band of white boys watching the game and he'd run into them. I was trying to decide whether or not to circle back and look for him when he strolled smiling out of the darkness and the trees. When I saw him grinning, I remembered to be mad.

"What the hell," I said. "Running like that."

"They weren't going to do anything to you," he said. "They just wanted some May McIntosh stories." His smile got bigger. He could see I didn't understand something. "Man, I didn't run away at all," he said. "I went far enough they couldn't find me, close enough to hear everything you said. You can't spot me in the dark."

"I made some of it up," I said. I needed to come clean about May McIntosh and the stories I told. I picked my bike off the tree and started walking it toward the road.

"How much?" Columbus said. I thought for a second and realized I couldn't remember all of the lies. They had evaporated quickly in the cold air. When I didn't answer right away, Columbus said, "Well, let me ask you this. Do all white girls taste like coconuts?"

We hit the sand road and I jumped on my seat, pushed down hard on the pedal. "Most of them," I said, and we rode off into the dark.

COLUMBUS AND I reached the intersection just beyond the school where I'd turn left and he'd head toward Nicholtown. Neither one of us stopped pedaling, just yelled over our shoulders that we'd see each other at school on Monday. The street-lights at the intersection gave way to more darkness for the last few blocks of the ride. The dogs that usually chased me in the daylight couldn't see me coming out of the night, and only one gave up a half-hearted yelp when he saw me zipping by.

Nobody had worried any about my being gone. My mother's night shift at the hospital wouldn't be over for another couple of hours, and my father's fishing bucket wasn't on the porch, which meant he was still off in a place where he was the only traveler. Down the hall, I saw the blue-glow of the television spilling out of the den, along with the sound of voices. I hadn't noticed my clothes until I stood in the doorway and Eli looked up. "What happened to you?" he said. My sneakers were black with swamp mud and the muck went up almost to my knees. I was glad my mother wasn't home.

"Nothing," I said and he knew I was lying, but he wouldn't say anything, because when it came right down to it, he didn't care. He was too deep into his show.

"It's an old John Wayne movie," he said. "You know, Daddy is wrong. John Wayne runs away a lot. He's been running from Indians most of this movie. And this woman's been causing a lot of trouble." On the screen, John Wayne galloped across the red desert, a band of mad Comanches on his heels. Riding with him, pressed tight against his side and holding on for all she was worth, was a dark-haired woman. She'd buried her head in his shoulder and her eyes were squeezed shut.

"But he knows where he's headed," I said. "That's the difference." I took my shoes to the bathroom and washed them off in the tub. My eyes felt heavy. There were too many people in the world hiding and running and sneaking looks at strangers—too much riding around in the dark, dodging dogs and streetlights. I heard gunshots from the den. Maybe John Wayne had taken a stand after all. I suddenly felt tired and older than really I was, and I knew tomorrow, the world wasn't going to make me feel any younger.

STAND-IN JESUS

ON EASTERS, OUR FATHER WAS LORD AND SAVIOR. This was because he had a beard and half a stomach. The long beard, more salt-and-pepper than anything else, hung almost to his belt and made him resemble those paintings of ancient prophets. The missing stomach turned him hollow-cheeked, with the dark-eyed expression of someone constantly persecuted. He could fill up on a bowl of soup and a handful of saltine crackers. All year long, he resembled a man who had been betrayed and chased down by Romans, but only during Easter did his bony face and sunken eyes become valuable to the church and community.

The rehearsals began always in early March. I remember my mother complaining about him acting in the church Easter pageant. She was a regular at church, but had little desire for pageantry. And casting my father as Jesus confused her. My guess is that she did not appreciate the irony of a non-church-going veteran portraying the Messiah. Maybe she thought it was religious payback. "I suppose you could say that God took half his stomach. Perhaps making your father a star is reparations." On the other hand, we thought it made perfect sense. What did we know? We were kids. It didn't take much to convince us. And despite all of her objections, she always ended up coming to the play, sitting in a pew near the back, watching her husband ultimately rise from the dead.

The fact is, God had nothing to do with my father's stomach. It was the Ho Chi Minh Trail instead. When the North Viet Cong decided to push south one fall, my father and his raggedy platoon were smack in the way. While they squatted on the shoulder of the washed-out ox path, under the banana leaves, shooting at shadows in black pajamas, my father drank a palmful of water from a mud puddle.

"It didn't seem stupid at the time," he said. "Of the stuff going on at that particular moment, drinking from a mud hole seemed like the last thing that would screw my life up." Some sort of rare Southeast Asian parasite was backstroking in the mud puddle one second, setting up shop in my dad's stomach lining the next. There was a family story that my father kept the parasite in a jar somewhere, swimming in formaldehyde. My brother and I searched every drawer and shelf we could reach on our own. We never found the war parasite. My father received a Purple Heart plus a government-paid operation to remove half his stomach before the parasite could go on an offensive toward the rest of his vital organs.

I HAVE SEEN pictures of my father in the times before the parasite and the war. He is big and soft, like a risen loaf of bread, like a man who has just been told a good joke. A smile always floats across his face in these photos. He looks as though he rarely missed meals. "One sip of brown water, and all this happens," he still said sometimes, shaking his head, still smiling. "And to think, I had a half full canteen on my belt."

They tell me it was difficult for my mother when he returned home. Not because he suffered from any of that Vietnam trauma you read about—the nightmares and the sweats and the general fear of living under a roof. My father never had any of those problems. When he came back, his problem turned out to be the half-stomach, and by the time of his homecoming, he had already taken on the expression of a starving man.

I've also seen the black-and-white photo of my mother, the one somebody took while my father was away. She props against the hood of a car—a Ford, I think—turned at a slight angle away from the camera. She looks beyond the photographer. You can see the curve of her hip, can see how beautiful and hopeful she was back then. I don't know which came first, the beauty or the hope. But she planned on marrying a doughy, smiling high school athlete she drove to Ft. Jackson one day in May, not the rail-thin, thin-lipped GI who stepped off the plane holding the stitches in his side. He still had that smile, but he was smiling about something else then, just happy to be away from mud puddles.

He supposedly spent weeks convincing her that the same man was, indeed, lurking inside that skin and bones. He finally won her over. I don't know if he charmed her or wore her down. A betting man would probably lay money on the latter. Who knows? The best I've been able to do is put bits and pieces together.

By the time my brother and I came along, my father had already established himself as the perennial Easter Jesus. And he perfected his role yearly, tweaking the subtleties of Christ. There wasn't another person in our town that could drag that cross down the road like him, shouldering that hunk of balsa wood, enduring the insults from the crowd. When he gazed down on the followers at the foot of the cross at the end of the second act, you would have thought life was truly draining from his sweaty body. I remember thinking one spring, during the play, that if my father had a whole stomach, there was no way they could've hoisted his big body up on that cross without a decent rope. So I decided then and there that drinking from the mud puddle in Vietnam was God's hand working His magic, making our father forget about the canteen and dip a scoop of brown, parasite-filled scum. There was a purpose at work, a reason that, year after year, he was resurrected and my mother complained.

We got by. He collected his veteran's disability checks and sold boxes of re-loaded shotgun shells. He'd walk through a dove field after a big shoot and gather up all the spent paper and plastic hulls. Then, he'd come home, sit at the hand re-loader, with its compartments for powder and shot, and he'd make shells all night long. I fell asleep most nights to the rhythmic *ca-chink* of the reloader. His price for a box of shells was a dollar fifty less than what you paid at McClary's Sporting Goods, so he had a pretty steady stream of business. Hank McClary was angry at first, but when he realized that it was a veteran and a stand-in Jesus trying to make a living on half a stomach, he actually began sending customers my father's way.

My mother was a part-time nurse then, working an assortment of odd shifts at the hospital in town. The days she didn't work were spent herding me and my brother to football practices and friends' houses. My father never did much of that. He was always at the games, but never at the practices. He said it wore him down too much now, watching young boys run around the football field. He told us, "I used to run like that. I was grease, man." But I knew that he was too round to be fast in his full-stomach days. Still, you could see from the dull gaze in his eyes that, in his case, sitting down to watch a football game was like looking in a mirror way too long. In the reflection, you start to see what you *used* to be. These days, he was a man who'd flutter away in a strong headwind like a thrown-out candy wrapper. No matter what the mirror said, he wasn't a linebacker any more.

WHAT WE REMEMBER and what we choose to forget is never up to us. If it was, we'd recall only the happiest moments of our lives, or perhaps those times when we realized beyond a shadow of a doubt that we were about to change forever, that nothing would ever be the same again. We'd only file away the good things. We'd forget the bad stuff: the Vietnams and the muddy water and the punishments and the girl who broke our heart. I would certainly choose to forget one particular Easter.

Easter came early that year, in March, which cut down considerably on the amount of rehearsal time for the play. (And I have to mention, when I say *play* I don't mean some little living room skit lit by flashlights. This was a full-blown production with make-up and sound effects and live music.)

We had people in our congregation who annually tried to buy their way into heaven. In the name of the Trinity, they purchased footlights and scenery and a full-size cross atop a fake Calvary. People drove from other churches for our Easter pageant. And they paid an admission. The Easter pageant financed new choir robes and a new gym floor.

"I don't see why you have to go to all the trouble of a play to make money. Why don't you just collect all the money it takes to *put on* a play and buy those new things anyway? Why go through all of that rehearsal and wasted time? I hate this time of year," my mother said, trying to make sense of religious bookkeeping.

"Because people would rather pay money for a dramatic Christian spectacle instead of a floor buffer," my father answered, the one and only time I ever heard him use the word 'spectacle' or 'dramatic.' Plus (I thought, but didn't add aloud) he'd lose one more thing he could actually do if he couldn't play Jesus once a year.

That spring, my brother and I, like always, portrayed street urchins on the road to Calvary. Our job was to cast aspersions. That's what Miss Burch, the director, told us. "Lean out into the road and cast aspersions at Christ."

So, without fear of punishment, we got to call our father names and spit in his general direction. As he struggled up the road with his fake-heavy cross, he gazed into our eyes and each year, without fail, as his back was turned slightly to the audience, he winked at us. When you're a kid and most of the Bible stories you hear are about fires and floods and mystery, having Jesus wink in your direction is a welcome miracle.

Miss Burch was feeling the pressure of an early Easter. She had us rehearsing twice on weekend days and all night long during the week. We'd arrive at the church with our father just after dark, after a quick supper at home, something we had to throw together because our mother refused to adjust her cooking schedule for the Easter pageant rehearsals. "If you want me to cook, be here at the usual supper time. If not, eat cereal and go pay for new organ pipes or whatever."

Most nights, we fell asleep during late rehearsals. All of us urchins did. We'd curl up behind the velvet backdrop like ignored cats until Miss Burch rustled us awake for the street scene. We'd still be rubbing our eyes and yawning when Christ lumbered by, bearing his burden.

Miss Burch had been directing Christian drama long enough to know when we were burning out. My father seemed even thinner than normal, what with missing meals and rehearsing his lines every night for hours and hours. We urchins cried for no reason other than the fact that we were constantly tired and underfed. My brother wanted to know if Miss Burch was doing this on purpose, to make us feel more like poor street people. I said I didn't think she was that smart.

When we were all about to crumble into whining piles of skin and bones, Miss Burch surprised us. On the Friday night before Easter Sunday—Good Friday night—we arrived for rehearsal. The sky was orange, I remember that. Orange and clear, like a fire was burning off in the distance, a fire so big, it lit the sky. We gathered around Miss Burch for our instructions. The adults sipped hot coffee they poured from the metal church urn. It was their way of staying awake. Miss Burch walked in front of us, her ankles spilling out of her shoes. Miss Burch was a large woman. My mother called her buxom once and Dad had to explain what "buxom" was. "Just look at her," he said of Miss Burch. "That's walking, talking buxom."

"How is everyone this evening?" she asked. Fines and Goods drifted around the room. "We've all been working so hard, I think we need to do something different tonight, something we haven't done yet." We groaned.

"I think we need to have a night off. Go home and watch television, take a walk outside. You can almost smell spring tonight, you know. Do something new, something other than rehearse a play. You see? This really is a good Friday." Miss Burch smiled without looking at anyone. "Go! Shoo! We'll run it again tomorrow. Relax. And I mean it! God bless us all!" She smiled once more, turned on a pudgy ankle and walked toward the rear of the stage, then disappeared into the dark skirts at the side.

Before I could find him, my father was at my ear. "Let's pick up a box of chicken for your momma."

"You don't eat chicken," my brother said.

"I can't eat much of anything, so it doesn't really matter, does it? You know how your momma loves fried chicken. Let's go, boys." He made a beeline for the door, his clothes struggling to find a grip on his body.

On the way home, my brother and I picked at hot, crusty chicken skin, eating our fill before we even hit the driveway. "Slow down, boys," my dad said. "Save some for the rest of us."

"You don't eat chicken," my brother said again. It had suddenly become his refrain for the night.

"Well, I might give it a try. Something new, right? Just like Miss Burch said," Dad answered, swinging the car on to our street. It was dark by then, the orange sky gone, and the stars beginning to come out. I could see the bright light on the side of our house.

I had my hand in the chicken bucket, hunting for another hunk of skin when my brother saw the car. I always remember he was the one to see it first. "Who's that?" he asked us.

He slowed down. A white Dodge sat in our driveway. I didn't know anyone who had a plain-looking car like that. I could feel my father going down the list of people he knew who drove white Dodges. "Aunt Louise. Didn't she buy a new car?" We couldn't answer, because, frankly, we didn't care who it was.

"We don't have enough chicken for Aunt Louise," my brother said. He has always tended to look out for himself. It was a trait that developed early and never really subsided.

"I can't eat chicken. She can have my share," my father said, perhaps still in character, exercising his Jesus-like goodness. He pulled in behind the Dodge.

When I've retold this story in other places and at other times, I sometimes embellish. Like, I'll say that our dad cut the lights at the corner and drifted silently to our driveway without being seen, like a spy or an undercover cop. I'll say that he didn't talk the whole time, suspicious from the moment he squinted at the white car. Or I'll even say that he searched the inside of the Dodge like a detective, combing for clues. But the fact of the matter is that he simply pulled in behind the Dodge, turned off our car, climbed out and headed for the door inside the garage. We were slow, struggling and arguing about who got to carry the chicken bucket and who was going to eat the drumsticks and "there is no way I am gonna eat chicken without no skin." That sort of thing.

We stood in the half-light of the open garage when we heard the yell. It echoed in the space, bouncing off the dark, unfinished walls. "Jesus H. Christ!" someone screamed. A man. A man with a deep voice. He could have sung in the choir with a voice that deep. "Jesus!" he boomed again. I remember thinking: he must recognize my father from his past appearances in the Easter play.

We stopped, both of us with death grips on the paper bucket. We heard the thumps and thuds of running. Someone was crying. I wanted to go near the door, near the glow from the inside, but then again, that was the last thing I wanted to do. My brother put a piece of chicken in his mouth. A man I didn't recognize filled the screen door in the garage for a second, stopped like he was readjusting his bearings, then flung the door open. He lumbered past us, carrying his coat like a football, instead of putting it on. I remember the slap of his bare feet on the cold cement floor. I didn't see any shoes. He looked right at us. "Goddamn it," he hissed. "Kids. I knew it."

I've never been able to decide if he was surprised we existed or if his sneer was a reaction to children in general. My brother chewed and I watched the door, waiting to see who would appear next.

"Goddamn it!" the man yelled from behind us. He was blocked in. I heard his car start smoothly, like the engine was new. He eased back a couple of feet, cut the wheels, then made a tight turn right through my mother's flowerbeds and the side yard. He destroyed everything he rolled over. He bounced over the curb and gunned it down the street, taking the turn at the corner too fast, the sounds of the whole event lingering long after the white Dodge was gone for good.

My mother appeared next in the doorway. "You've brought some chicken." She sang the words instead of saying them. Her voice was too happy.

"Who was that?" I asked her.

"It wasn't Aunt Louise," my brother said.

"Nobody," my mother answered. "It's just somebody. Visiting. Nothing to worry about." She tugged on the clip at the back of her hair. "Nobody really. Let's eat." She waved us toward the light in the kitchen. Before we reached the door, my father appeared behind her.

"Boys," he said, "I have to go back to the church. Something I forgot." He patted each of us on the top of our head. He didn't say a word to my mother. She watched him, but he wouldn't give her a glance. He stopped for a second on his way to the car, surveying the damage to the grass and the flowers. When he turned back to us, he said, "Don't wait on me. I don't eat the chicken anyway."

THAT WAS GOOD Friday. The next morning, my father woke us and drove us to Easter pageant practice, but just dropped us off. "I've already talked to Miss Burch. You all are going to rehearse without Jesus today. Something I've got to take care of."

Miss Burch read all of Jesus' lines, which sounded funny—a woman saying those words. We only practiced a single run-through that morning. Miss Burch pronounced us ready as we'd ever be and reminded us what time to be at the church for the performance the next day. "We have to put make-up on everybody, so get here in plenty of time. And pray. Don't forget to pray," she said. Miss Burch was sweating slightly; the effort of directing *and* playing Jesus had clearly exhausted her.

The rest of that day and into the night, I remember my father wandering in and out of our house. Suddenly, he would be looming at the door of our room, as much as a man that thin can loom, then silently he would disappear, as if he had lost so much weight, he didn't make any sounds when he moved. We would see him outside, walking the property line of our little front yard, stopping when he reached the chewed up grass and flowerbeds. He never *said* anything, just stared with those round, sunken-in eyes, soaking in everything he saw.

My mother spent the day bustling: cleaning, sewing, writing thank-you notes for one reason or the other. She made a couple of calls to relatives. She even put on a bandanna, climbed into the attic and attacked the stacks of boxes and rolls of old, unlaid carpet. Once, she grabbed a shovel and wheelbarrow and headed for the place the guy in the Dodge tore up. My dad met her outside and sent her back in before she started digging. They maybe said three words to each other the whole afternoon.

Easter Sunday came up clear and chilly, one of those days that exists simply to remind you not to think too far ahead toward warmer weather. Spring might be coming, but in its own time. My father drove us to the church. Mom stayed at the house. No one said a word. Finally, I asked anyone who would listen about being nervous.

"Nervous 'bout what?" my brother said. He didn't have enough sense to be nervous. The crowds that would soon be spilling out into the hallways and parking lots had no effect on him. He maintained his own little world. Population one.

"Nothing to be nervous about, son," Dad answered, his voice calm and deeper than normal, like he had the beginning of a cold.

"All them people—" I started.

"Those people," he corrected.

"All those people, just watching us," I said.

"Don't worry about what they're doing. Remember what Miss Burch says. Just think about what you're supposed to do, not what might go wrong." He smiled at me. "Keep a positive thought."

WE GOT OUR make-up, smelly stuff so thick you could write your name on your cheek. Actually, that's what my brother did, watching himself in the mirror while he carved his initials on his face. Nobody seemed to mind or notice. I parted the curtain once to take a look, and a rush of heat blew in from the audience. So many bodies jammed into one auditorium, they hummed like a hive on the other side of the curtain.

The play went as good as ever. My father had the disciples over for the Last Supper. He boomed out his prediction that somebody would betray him. He walked in the Garden, which was actually some donated latticework from the hardware store with plastic grapes painted to make them look like olives. We had our little scene when we cast aspersions. Jesus stumbled by, hugging that balsa wood cross. The real one, the one the other actors eventually nailed him to, was made of four-by-fours, too heavy to drag down our make-believe road. Only thing, he didn't wink at us this particular year. He looked right down on us, and I waited, but no wink.

Finally, we came to one of the big, quiet scenes, when my father was balanced on the little platform against the cross, his arms spread out wide like a giant bird, the fake blood dripping from dark spots on his hands and ankles. At his feet, the faithful waited. He only had the one line here: "Forgive them Father, they know not what they do."

Miss Burch told us that this was the true climax of the entire drama, that the resurrection was all falling-off action after this forgiveness scene. She always had my dad play it up big. "Scan the crowd. Roll your eyes back in your head a time or two. Try to talk, but have trouble getting it out. Croak a little. Get them in the palm of your hand, then let them have it." That was how Miss Burch directed. She called it "tease 'em and please 'em."

But my father wasn't scanning the crowd at all. His eyes were squeezed shut inside those dark circles, the lines on his face drawn taut and deep. He was either thinking or dying. The crowd shifted in their seats. From where I watched among the urchins and townspeople, I could tell the audience was wondering if this was part of the play or not. Jesus opened his eyes quickly and the crowd gasped a little, like it scared them. I knew he had them in that place, in the palm of his hand. I waited for the line. We all waited. And it didn't come.

From my right, I heard Miss Burch prompting him. "Forgive. It's forgive them, Faaaa…" she whispered.

Jesus said nothing. He sighed deeply. One of the faithful at his feet hissed toward the curtain, "Give him a line!" Miss Burch prompted again.

My father focused on the audience a little, his eyes now drawn into narrow slits. I turned and looked where he looked. He had drawn a bead on the far wall, near the tall, stained-glass windows. All I could see were silhouettes. People of all sizes. A few ladies in hats. One of the hats caught in the yellow glare of the window frame was the one my mother wore every Easter to watch her children and her husband in the Easter pageant. I knew by her shadow it was my mom. She always showed up.

Miss Burch hissed, "It's 'forgive!'"

Another one of the faithful at the foot of the cross tried to ad lib and shake my father from his daze. "Forgive us all, Lord. Please!" he called up at the cross, but he didn't get a response. The audience was beginning to rumble. I could see people out there in the dark talking to each other, wondering why Jesus wasn't talking.

But on this day, Jesus didn't say a word about forgiveness from the cross. He stared a hole through the wall lined with the hats. He shook his head slightly. Then, he simply closed his eyes and let his head drop.

The play churned forward. Dad did fine with the resurrection and the meeting with one of the Marys and with Peter. We had a big finish and a loud curtain call, but I heard some people afterward at the refreshment tables say they were a little let down. "If I'm going to drive all this way, the least He could do is forgive everybody," one man said, shoving a cookie in his mouth.

My mother found us at a table covered with pound cakes. She told us we did a good job and we should go home now. "Easter is over," she said.

"But Daddy forgot a line," my brother said.

"No, no he didn't. He just played it a different way," she answered. "You can ride with me now. Your father will be along when he's ready."

He did come home, not long after we'd parked in the garage. We ate dinner that night, all four of us around the table. We went to bed at the usual time. The next day, another week started, then another month. Soon, another season, another spring. It just went on. Church, school, vacations. Life didn't stop because my father dropped his line. Didn't stop because of the man who drove a white Dodge through our grass. In fact, as hard as I try, I cannot recall hearing my parents ever talk about that barefoot man in front of me and my brother. He became a ghost or a magic trick. I guess they worked it out amongst themselves when we weren't around or while we slept. They must have decided to say all there was to say and be done with it. Or say absolutely nothing and let the silence fill up our house like an odor you can't identify. Back then, we were too young or too stupid to care about who he was or why he was. And now that my brother and I understand, too much time has passed us by.

The tire ruts in our yard turned to mud during spring thunderstorms that came up a few weeks after Easter, but my brother and I never even considered drinking the brown water. That fall, my father sprigged in new grass to cover up the holes. And the spring after that, he told our church to look for a new kind of Jesus.

THE ESSO
TRIFECTA

EMERSON MCGILL'S ESSO STATION WAS ROBBED ON A Thursday afternoon. A man Mr. McGill said was even shorter than him walked in at closing time with pantyhose pulled over his head and asked for all the money in the register and a carton of Camel hard packs.

"I don't think he could see too good through that underwear," Mr. McGill said the next afternoon when I came by to roll my newspapers. Each day, the truck from Charleston dropped off the *Evening Post* just after lunch. Once school was over, I'd pedal to the Esso station on the big English racing bike my uncle gave me, the one my father converted into a paperboy special, with a huge wire basket on the front and high handlebars. Mr. McGill helped me with the papers every afternoon before my route. Some days, when I pulled up after school, he already had half of them rolled and stacked on the cement island near the gas pumps. It was my job to shut down the pumps every evening after my route. Mr. McGill was, for the most part, too drunk from a day of Old Crow and Sprite to remember. He paid me five dollars a week to keep folks from stealing free gas after dark. We had a deal.

Now that it was summer and I didn't have school to worry about, I got to the Esso earlier in the day. If I pedaled hard, I could finish my route and still have time to head to the river before dark and fish or swim or watch the high school kids go parking at the turnaround on the sand road that led into the swamp. I'd heard about the robbery that morning from my mother. "I'm not sure about you going to the station today," she said. "There might be aftermath."

I wasn't completely clear what she meant by aftermath, and when I pulled up to the Esso station, everything looked the same. No police cars, no broken glass, no chalk lines on the asphalt. Mr. McGill sat as usual, under the shade of the awning, on an empty, upturned bucket that used to hold the powdery stuff he spread on oil spills. The batch of newspapers lay stacked beside him. He'd already rolled a dozen or so. His coffee mug was within reach, next to the box of thin, green rubber bands.

"You heard?" he said when I parked my bike.

"Sort of," I said. My mother knew none of the details. Mr. McGill filled me in about the pantyhose and the short guy.

"He even had a little gun," he said. "You'd think a little guy would want a bigger gun."

He said there was only thirty-five dollars in the register. "He didn't know what he was doing. He coulda grabbed things in the garage he could sell for hundreds. The air drill. The battery charger. You can pawn those in Sumter for good coin. I'm starting to think he isn't real good at robbing folks."

I rolled papers twice as fast as Mr. McGill. He spent too much time getting the folds perfect before he slid a rubber band to the center with his tiny fingers. I told him a couple of times a week that he didn't have to help me, but he said he liked doing it. He said he liked having an easy job he could finish.

He'd packed a big dip in his lower lip, which was new. He saw me staring when he spit over his shoulder. "Zona wants me to quit smoking," he said. "This is what I like to call marital compromise." He spit again, but I don't think he needed to.

Mr. McGill's wife was named after the state of Arizona. She was six feet tall and flat-footed. She never smiled. Other than the rare time she'd drop by the Esso station, I only saw them together at church, Zona towering over Mr. McGill, the two of them like a schoolteacher and a puny kindergarten kid. They came to church on communion Sundays and Easter. My mother said that was the only time God took attendance, anyway.

Mr. McGill stopped rolling. He sipped from his coffee mug. "You know," he said, "it's probably like lightning striking." He paused, waiting, I guess, for me to carry my weight in the conversation, but I wasn't sure which direction he was headed.

"Lightning," I said back.

"What I mean is, you get struck by lightning, your chances of getting hit again are pretty damn small. So now that I've been robbed, it probably won't ever happen again." He spit from his bottom lip and I wondered how he kept the Old Crow and Sprite and Bumblebee dip-spit from all mixing together into some sort of toxic brew inside his mouth. I thought I might throw up thinking about it.

"But, you know, I'm not taking any chances," he said. "People do get struck by lightning twice, I hear. Come on back when you're done with the papers, before you turn off the pumps, and I'll show you what I got in mind. I been thinking on this."

I couldn't imagine the man with the pantyhose on his face showing up in the county again, much less at McGill's Esso. He was hundreds of miles away by now, or at the very least, holed up somewhere back in the swamp, smoking Camels and drinking all the Miller High Life thirty-five dollars could buy.

When I finished rolling—and Mr. McGill finished talking—I layered the papers in my basket and took off on my route. I could finish in two hours if I hustled. I had somewhere around sixty customers, but most of them lived pretty close to one another. There were four machines on my route too. That's where I made most of my money, in the machines. Unlocking the back of those machines in the afternoons was like breaking a rusty lock on a treasure chest. They were always full of change, especially the ones outside the Kingstree Inn and the IGA grocery. I could never figure out why all those people using the machines didn't just get a subscription and let me sling a paper on their driveway every day, but I didn't complain, as long as they kept shoving quarters and nickels and dimes in the little slots.

The Inn was my last stop of the day. After I refilled the machine with fresh, flat papers and emptied the change tray, I sat at the counter in the diner off the lobby and had a jelly doughnut from under the glass case, along with a fountain Coke. Marlene was the afternoon waitress. Sometimes she charged me, but sometimes she'd say, "I been known to trade a doughnut for news of the world," which meant I'd eat free if

I left a *Charleston Evening Post* on the counter.

But I had no time for a doughnut. I was supposed to head back to the Esso station after I finished up. I hoped Marlene looked a little hurt when I pedaled by and waved through the big window of the restaurant. Sometimes Marlene's waitress uniform puckered just to the right of where she pinned her nametag. She wore colored bras. The only kind I'd seen around my house were my mother's white ones that hung in the bathroom. I didn't know that bras were any other color than white until I became a paperboy.

I couldn't spot Mr. McGill when I pulled up. He wasn't sitting in the wicker chair in the shade of the garage. I heard a thin, metallic rasp when I leaned my bike against a pump, and inside the office, Mr. McGill squatted like a gas station gnome in front of the glass candy case, sawing at something between his legs. Scraps of shelving lumber and finishing nails littered the floor. A tape measure, the kind my mother kept in her sewing kit, coiled at his feet like a skinny snake. A drip of sweat dangled from the tip of Mr. McGill's nose.

"I'm building a surprise," he said without looking up at me. "Get yourself a PayDay if you want. I'm almost at a stopping place."

I grabbed a candy bar from the other side of the case and put it in the soda box to cool it down a little. I didn't know what was going on. He had plenty of shelves already. The walls were lined with tiny bottles of gas treatment and lubricants. I didn't see room for more stuff.

"What's the surprise?"

He finally turned around and grinned. "Oh, it's loud," he said. He put a couple of extra nails between his lips while he banged one into the shelving board. In a few minutes, he'd constructed what looked like two sides of a long, narrow box. The joints were neat and dovetailed.

"You're pretty good at that," I said.

He grinned again. "I worked construction in the Army," he said. "I was too little to fight. That's what they said, at least. I got assigned to carpentry."

"I didn't know you went in the Army."

"The Army ain't much of a conversation starter. I did meet Zona when I was building things for my country. I guess that's something," he said.

By the time I'd shoved the last cold piece of the PayDay in my mouth, I could see what Mr. McGill was up to. He'd constructed a secret compartment mounted in the corner of the glass case, directly beneath the drawer of the cash register. The compartment fit tightly against the top and side of the case with some right angle mounts. Mr. McGill could stand behind the register and reach into the new compartment without anyone seeing what he was grabbing. But from the front of the case, it would look like Mr. McGill was reaching straight into his cash drawer. It was illusion, sleight of hand.

"Surprise," Mr. McGill said. "That's it for the night. I'll finish up tomorrow sometime. I'm taking off." It was almost dark, and Mr. McGill was never at the station when evening came on. He never thought about his pumps. While he put his tools away, I felt like I had just witnessed something important, but I wasn't sure what it was. His coffee mug wasn't anywhere in sight.

THERE WAS NO school, so I used the mornings to count my money from the day before. I sorted the coins from the paper machines into dollar stacks and put the amounts into a little notebook I kept in a bank deposit bag. I had to be organized because twice a month, a woman from Charleston drove up to McGill's in an *Evening Post* panel van, and I handed over all of the collections from people on my route, plus a percentage from the paper machines. The left-over was mine to keep. Mr. McGill called me a newspaper slave one day, told me I wasn't bringing in enough money to make it worth my time, but I didn't mind. I always ended up with something in my pocket when the math was done. And Miss DeWitt, the one who drove the van up from Charleston, told me I was doing a fine job, and the people in Charleston were very happy with my performance, which I didn't believe. People in Charleston didn't really care how anybody in my town performed, one way or the other. But I always smiled at her when she said it. I was a good employee.

The morning after Mr. McGill built his little secret shelf in the candy case, my mother walked into my room, still in her nurse's uniform. She was sucking on a popsicle, so I knew she'd been to the grocery store after her shift ended early that morning. She always ate popsicles after she'd been to the IGA and stocked up on things for me and my brother. She never shopped for my old man. His stomach problems didn't allow for him to eat much of anything that wasn't the consistency of turkey gravy, and for that matter, I don't think he was around much the summer everything went down at McGill's.

She stood in the doorway, eating fast so the purple wouldn't drip on her uniform. "I can't let you start your paper route at the Esso station anymore. I wouldn't be a good mother if I did."

"What are you talking about?" I said. "That's where they

drop off the papers. Did you look at the machine when you were at the IGA? Have I sold a lot yet?" I knew that if the afternoon paper from the day before wasn't sold by eight o'clock the next morning, it would end up in the trash can.

"I'm bothered by the robbery," she said.

"The guy ain't stealing papers," I said. "Plus, that's over with."

Thinking back, I believe she knew she was leading me on, and she was enjoying the experience as much as the popsicle. "You haven't heard, have you? That's what you get for sleeping late. The world begins without you."

I looked up from my coins. "Heard what?"

She took a long slurp on the popsicle. "That guy came back again. This morning, when Emerson opened the station. Walked right in again with the hose on his face and took everything out of the cash register. Took Emerson completely by surprise."

I wanted to tell her that taking Mr. McGill by surprise wasn't exactly newsworthy, but I knew that wouldn't help matters any. "The same guy?" I asked. "At the same place?"

"Pretty brazen, I'd say."

"I need to go down there," I said, rising up from the bed. The stacks of coins collapsed onto the quilt.

"No, now, that's just what I'm talking about. Don't go near that place. I think I ought to forbid you."

I cocked my head like she'd spoken a foreign language. My mother's way wasn't to forbid anyone to do anything. She'd much rather let all of us—all of the men in her life— screw up, then fix our own messes, as long as she got to supervise the cleanup. I'd seen her do that with my father. It didn't seem like a very efficient system.

"I just want to see if Mr. Emerson's okay," I said. I knew that would appeal to the compassionate nurse in her.

"Just don't linger," she answered. The popsicle was gone and she was down to the purple-stained stick. I hit the bottom of the steps when she called after me, "You shouldn't leave all your money out. There are bad people around!"

The Esso station looked abandoned from a block away. Nobody parked at the pumps. I didn't even see Mr. McGill's pickup anywhere. I found him inside the office, pacing between the Coke cooler and an empty glass case.

"Can you believe that? Same little bastard, wearing the same panty on his head," he said, marching a straight line like a sentry and spinning on his heel when he reached the cooler. "He took every single carton of cigarettes. Oh, and all the change for the day. Almost fifty dollars."

Before I could ask Mr. McGill why he thought the guy had come back, he answered the question for me. "He knew I wouldn't expect him. He banked on me figuring he was long gone. He may not look smart with that panty on his face, but I tell you, he has a razor sharp criminal mind. And you know, I was twenty minutes from outsmarting him." He stopped his pacing and stood in front of the glass case. "If he'd come twenty minutes later..." His voice trailed off and he motioned at me to come closer. "Twenty damn minutes."

Mr. McGill pointed in the general direction of his new secret shelf. I bent down to look. When my eyes finally focused, I saw the outline of a shelf—a new, dark compartment he'd built the afternoon before. Inside the compartment, I saw a pair of circles, too close together to be eyes, but perfectly round. Mr. McGill walked behind the register, reached below the drawer and, from inside the secret compartment, pulled out a sawed-off double barrel. It looked like maybe a 16 gauge. He slid it back in its hiding place. I didn't like looking into loaded barrels of anything. I jumped back from the case.

"If he'd come twenty minutes later, when that little bastard asked me for all the money in the drawer, I'd have reached under here and pulled the trigger and taken out most of his midsection." I heard a click. "He'd a never known where it came from. A surprise. I filed the triggers so both barrels go off at the same time. Double surprise."

That afternoon a sheriff's deputy pulled up while Mr. McGill and I rolled papers. He parked close enough that he could talk from inside his cruiser while we took papers off the big stack. Mr. McGill spit from his bottom lip before he talked. "You find that little bastard?" he said.

The deputy was a young guy I'd never seen before. He was new to our town, and his cruiser was spotless, like he'd hosed off every speck of dust that morning. He didn't take his eyes off me when he answered. "No sign. Still at large."

"I don't see how he could just disappear," Mr. McGill said. He started to reach for his mug but thought better of it, with a cop in front of him.

"You deliver every day?" The deputy was talking to me now. I thought: He's new. Maybe he wants a subscription.

"Every day but Sunday," I said. "*Evening Post* doesn't have a Sunday paper. It's a buck fifty a week. I collect on the first and third Saturdays of the month."

"I don't want a paper, kid," he said. He swung his door open. When he stepped out, I could see he was big. The rolled-up sleeves on his khaki sheriff's uniform strained tight against his arms. He probably lifted weights when he wasn't being a cop.

"Oh for shit's sake, Wesley," Mr. McGill said. "You been reading too many police manuals."

I was confused, like I'd been dropped into a half-done conversation. And I was surprised that somebody that big was named Wesley. It sounded like a smaller name.

"Wife gets killed, look at the husband. Store gets robbed, look at somebody who knows the owner. Policing one-oh-one," Wesley said.

"I don't get it," I said. I had stopped rolling papers.

Mr. McGill reached for his mug and took a long swallow. Wesley's eyes were still locked on me. "He thinks you were the one what robbed me," he said. "Twice."

"I wouldn't rob you!" I stood up quickly, and Wesley could see how tall I was for my age. "My mother was the one that told me about what happened."

"Wesley, get back in your fancy car and get on your radio and start telling everybody to look for a guy the size of a first grader. He's probably got a panty in his back pocket and that little pea-shooter pistol tucked in his crotch, and when you find him, don't even bring him back here, just take him out in the swamp and cut him loose. He'll get eaten up by something before morning." He took another sip. "But don't come around here accusing the paperboy because you've been watching every episode of *Hawaii Five-O*. This ain't Hawaii."

"You say your mother knew what happened?" Wesley said. He reached into his back pocket and pulled out a notebook.

"Get out of my station," Mr. McGill said and jumped off his bucket. He pushed Wesley back into his car.

I'd never seen anyone touch a policeman like that. And I'd never been accused of a crime. My face burned. I felt dangerous for a few seconds, like I might really be able to do something wrong.

Wesley pulled away quickly. He tried to smoke the tires when he hit the street, but the car coughed and lurched when Wesley punched the gas.

"Those points need to be reset. Car that clean on the outside ought to run smoother," Mr. McGill said, sitting back down on his bucket.

TWO SATURDAYS A month, I collected from all my customers. Most of them remembered to leave the money in their mailboxes or thumbtacked to their front doors. All I had to do was gather up the envelopes. But there were always a half-dozen or so people I had to chase down, people who didn't remember what Saturday meant in the paper route business.

Miss Byrd, who had been my third-grade teacher at Kingstree Elementary, was so old and addled, I wasn't sure why she still ordered the paper. Every time I'd ring her bell and remind her it was Saturday, she received the news like I was a fortune teller presenting secret information. Then, I'd have to remind her she had to actually pay for the papers I threw on her porch every day. But she handed me the money and probably forgot ten minutes later why she was missing a few dollars from the little red handbag she always swung on her forearm.

Clarence Harrell's was another bell I had to ring. He spent his Saturdays watching television in a blue terrycloth bathrobe. He lived alone at the end of Green Street, the final house on my route. My mother said Clarence's wife left him when their kids went off to college, because the two of them didn't have anything left to worry about at that point. He owned the biggest color television I had ever seen. On Saturdays when I came to collect, he made me step inside the house and sit on the couch and watch the big TV while he hunted around for money. The television was the size of the Coke cooler at the Esso station. Clarence Harrell was one of those guys who, from the outside, looked like he might drink too much and live in a pup tent under a county bridge, but his house was huge, and I never smelled liquor on him the way I did with Mr. McGill.

This Saturday was no different. I came to the house on Green, grabbed the last paper out of my basket and headed for the door. It was cracked a bit. I heard Clarence yell from inside. "Come on in. I can't leave the television right now."

I knew my way to the den, and there sat Clarence in his usual robe, rubber shower shoes under his yellow feet. His recliner was cranked down, and he hunched forward, staring into the screen. "You follow horse racing?" he said.

On the screen, slick, dark race horses paraded around a dirt track. The colors on the screen hypnotized me immediately. The camera pushed in on one horse that pranced and pulled against its handler. "Oh, she's a little anxious," Clarence said, as if he were talking about a relative. "I can't go looking for your money right now. I got to watch this race. Sit down." He motioned to the couch.

Several newspapers that weren't the *Evening Post* lay open on the table beside his recliner, as well as a notebook and a few pencils sharpened down to the last couple of inches. He tapped the floor with one of the shower shoes. I could smell that some-thing had been fried in the last day or so. Fish sticks, maybe.

"You know what's happening here, right?" he asked with-out pulling his focus away from the screen. "You follow horse racing?" he repeated.

"Sure," I told him, and it wasn't quite a lie. I didn't follow horse racing, but I did read the sports pages of the *Evening Post*. I hadn't been a paper reader until I started delivering them. Now, I'd save a day-old copy from a machine and bring it home after my route. I'd spread the pages out on the kitchen table and pore over them. I liked obituaries, liked reading about lives I didn't know coming to an end. The comics bored me. The sports pages were all right. Most of the articles the last week or so had been about a horse named Canonero II. He'd won the Kentucky Derby and the Preakness and was supposed to win at Belmont this afternoon. I'd read articles about how the horse had shown up in Kentucky from Argentina, and nobody gave him much respect, and he won going away.

There had been articles about his jockey, a little Argentinean named Avila, who was about as unknown as the horse. The paper ran a picture of Avila one day. He was tiny as a cartoon. I thought about McGill's robber and wondered if he was perhaps a jockey that had turned to small crime.

When Canonero II won the Preakness, it was probably a bigger surprise to everybody, but now—today—he wasn't a secret anymore. The article I read on Friday said the crowd at Belmont was predicted to be the largest ever. The writer said it would be filled with people speaking Spanish. Clarence had been reading the same articles.

"They say Canonero's got a foot infection, but I don't

believe it," he said. "I think somebody's just trying to pull the money away from him. Started a rumor about a foot infection." For the first time, he turned toward me. "Can horses even get foot infections? I mean, they don't have toes."

I tried not to look down at Mr. Harrell's shower shoes. I'd read something about the horse and his infection, and it sounded like the truth to me, but I kept my mouth shut. I was there for my collection.

The closer to the paddock the horses moved, the more nervous Clarence became. He picked up one of his little pencils and chewed on the good end. "That's right. Rumor. I put all my money on Canonero even *after* I heard about that damn foot infection. Got to be a rumor. You a betting man?" he said.

I had no idea *where* anybody would bet on horse races in Kingstree, but I didn't doubt that it could happen. My father put money down on college football games now and then when he had cash to lose to his friends. He bought parlay cards a couple times a year, too, from the liquor store. I wanted to sound older when I answered Clarence. I thought about the day before, when Wesley suspected me of pulling off robberies. Maybe I was growing up.

"I don't shy away from a little action," I said, repeating a line I'd probably heard on television, some show like *Hawaii Five-O*. My answer surprised Clarence.

"You don't say?" He reached for his little notebook. "How much you carrying in that little bag of yours? Or maybe I should say, how much you willing to put on a horse?"

Now I was the surprised one. I didn't know how to bet on horse races. In the paper, I'd read about things like trifectas and exactas and betting the box. And I didn't have money to burn. I thought about the stacks of coins that collapsed on the bed. Miss DeWitt was driving up from Charleston on Monday to get her money, and I didn't want to disappoint her or those mysterious people in Charleston who supposedly admired my performance.

"I don't know, Mr. Harrell," I said and he cut me off with a wave and a snort.

"Just what I thought. Big talker."

I probably had somewhere in the neighborhood of fifty dollars in cash collections in the deposit bag. And I had all the change from the paper machines in there too, maybe five bucks. I decided I could part with the machine money.

"I probably got five dollars," I said.

"Son, you been collecting for the paper all afternoon. You got a bag full of money. Five dollars won't make you sweat. If you're going to bet, you got to have risk to make you sweat. That's what makes it fun. You got to bet enough, you feel the pain if you lose. And if you win, you feel like a thief what got away clean. That's what betting is all about. Skin in the game. But I get it. You're just a kid."

I was a kid with fifty bucks in cash bulging inside a bank deposit bag. Clarence could no longer sit still. The horses had circled the track, led by a stable hand on a second horse. Clarence started walking laps too, around his den. "You know how much money I got on that horse from south of the border? You don't want to know—that's how much," he said. His robe had come open and I could see bright boxer shorts, almost like the silks the jockeys wore on the color television.

The horses reached the paddock and lined up to be loaded. The camera focused on Canonero II. He looked calm, almost bored with all the activity around him. "That's what I like to see," Clarence said, "nice and easy. Save all that energy. If you want to lay some money down, you got about forty-five seconds. You can't bet on Canonero. I got him to win."

I wouldn't have bet on Canonero anyway. I didn't believe the horse could pull off a surprise three times in a row. Two surprises was nearly a miracle. It seemed like an impossible, almost insane task. "I don't know about any of the other horses," I said.

"Tell you what," he said, stopping his pacing, "I'll give you the field. Any horse except Canonero wins, you double what's in your bag. If mine wins, I get your Saturday collections." He smiled and for the first time ever, I noticed the gap between his front teeth. "Skin in the game, son." The smile wasn't friendly. It didn't match his eyes, which darted nervously in his face, like he was about to start running around the room.

I opened the deposit bag and turned my back while I counted my money. Forty-eight fifty. I felt pretty good about my odds. I didn't see any reason why horses couldn't get foot infections.

I'd never bet money on anything before. I wasn't ready for the heavy, metallic ache in my stomach when the final horse was stuffed into the paddock, and my bet went down, officially. Once it had dollar signs in front of it, the field didn't look so strong.

Clarence reached across to me and stuck out his hand for a shake, and I grabbed it, limply if I remember. "You got the field," he said. "Sucker." When he let go, I leaned toward the television and turned up the volume. The announcer's tinny voice poured out of the little speaker with a Christmas-morning excitement coating his words. He recited the horses' names one last time. I felt suddenly nauseated as the ache worked its way toward my feet. I shoved the deposit bag between my knees and squeezed it there. Clarence perched on the edge of his recliner.

I don't remember the bell ringing because there was a sudden rushing in my ears, like all the blood inside me trying to find a new path out, and I watched the horses bunch and scramble into the first turn. I could barely make out the now-faraway announcer who sounded as if he were yelling at us from inside a closet down the hall.

Clarence growled at the television. "Wire to wire, baby!" And he pointed at the screen. "Canonero's already at the front." He turned to me and I swear his eyes had gone red. I waited for foam to appear at the corners of his mouth. "Your field ain't looking so swift."

I squeezed my knees tighter and looked around for something I could throw up into, the taste of a sour stomach working its way up my throat. I thought about how I could make up the difference when I had to pay Miss DeWitt, started thinking about how maybe Mr. McGill would float me a loan. Then I remembered the robberies and figured he was running a little short. I couldn't tell my mother about betting. She would just laugh and tell me to wipe up this particular mess on my own.

The horses swam in front of my eyes. Canonero II hit the back stretch holding onto his lead, and Clarence's feet stomped in place as he bounced on his recliner, like he was running right alongside the horse. Then something happened. I think I might've noticed it before Clarence did. The lead began to shrink a few inches at a time. A couple of horses crept up on either side of Canonero II. Suddenly, it was like Avila threw out an anchor and the pair of horses swept past Canonero and each took a half-length lead—at least that's what the man on the television said. Canonero's stride even changed. He suddenly had a tiny hitch on one side. *Foot infection*, I thought. Things quickly had focus. I saw the horses clearly. The brightest of the silks came burning through the screen. The announcer was in my ear, telling me how Canonero had faded beyond recovery, how the distance was too much for him, how he'd never had to run a mile and half in South America, and I waited for him to add, *And this is America, by God*, but he didn't.

Canonero finished fourth, which isn't bad unless you're trying to win a Triple Crown. Clarence didn't glance at me, just kept his eyes glued on his big screen, like what he'd seen was a tease, a television dream that wouldn't be real when we all woke up. I did math in my head, wondering what I could buy with an extra forty-eight fifty. I felt stronger all of the sudden. I could have lifted that recliner Clarence slumped into.

"Dammit," was what he finally said in almost a whisper, then recovered a bit. "Oh well, risk and reward." He took his nub of a pencil and did some scribbling in his notebook. "I don't reckon you'd take a check," he asked, and I swear I didn't shake my deposit bag on purpose, but when he heard the rattle of coins, he took that for an answer. "Right. I wouldn't do business in nothing but cash either. I'll be right back."

While I waited for Clarence to return with my winnings, I watched Canonero cool down on the track. The camera spent more time on him than on the horse that had spoiled his Triple Crown, a light-colored one named Pass Catcher. Canonero didn't seem all that upset that he had probably disappointed the whole of South America. Avila was stunned, his head hung down low on his silks. Canonero's ears were up.

He was unaffected. That's how you need to handle bad things, I thought. That's the look you need when you lose. Like nothing ever happened.

Clarence counted out the money into my hand—most of it in fives and ones. "Now get outta my house, you little thief," he said, and I couldn't tell if he was kidding. The smile was gone.

"You still owe me for the paper. It's still Saturday," I said. I didn't want any of my horse money to pay for Clarence's *Charleston Evening Post*. He grumbled low in his chest and reached inside the pocket of his robe. The newspaper money had been tucked there the whole time. He was hoping I wouldn't ask for it.

"Better make your goddamn getaway," he said. "Come on back during football season. Give me a chance to make my money back." He pointed toward the front door and slumped down in his chair. On the screen, somebody'd draped a rose blanket on Pass Catcher's back. The last thing I heard Clarence say before I closed the front door sounded like a lot like "foot infection."

I was running later than normal for a Saturday, but I was richer, so time quit mattering. How many other things change when you got cash in your pocket? I headed back to McGill's Esso to turn off the pumps. From Clarence Harrell's house to the station was a slight uphill, and I could usually feel it in my legs at the end of an afternoon, but today the bike seemed to pedal itself.

Saturday was always a drunker day for Mr. McGill because he knew he had an entire Sunday to recover. His tall wife didn't make him go to church anymore because his snoring was loud enough to annoy the Christians. I remembered he owed me five dollars for a week of turning the pumps off at night. It seemed like my money was breeding more money, and I realized how rich people always got richer. I pedaled faster toward the far end of town. I'd have to pick up my money from Mr. McGill on Monday. I was sure he'd already locked up the office and headed for home.

I came around the bend in Longstreet Street and saw too many cars parked at the Esso station. It looked like they had pulled in from several directions at once. One of the cars was Wesley's spotless cruiser. Its lights were on, blue and blinking, but no siren. I didn't recognize the other cars, but they were serious-looking automobiles, all dark colors, all Fords. Some yellow tape fluttered across the doorway to the office. Mr. McGill's tall wife stood on the other side of it, like she was trapped. But when I pulled up, Zona ducked under, carrying her husband's coffee mug in her hand. It looked to be in a couple of large pieces.

Wesley fixed his eyes on me just like he had the day before. "This is a crime scene, paperboy," he said. I had no idea why Wesley hated me. Some people just don't click, I suppose.

I was scared to look into the office. I was sure they'd found the secret shelf and the sawed-off 16 gauge. I expected blood and body parts. As short as Mr. McGill said the robber stood, the blast might've taken his shoulders off. I didn't want to see what had happened when two barrels of buckshot came through the candy case and surprised somebody.

Wesley told me to go home, that there was nothing to see, but I couldn't look away, and I didn't put any pressure on my pedals. I peered inside the door and the tall wife came over and stood by me. I could tell she'd been crying. Her face sagged.

"Where is he?" I said. I wanted Mr. McGill to come out from behind the counter and tell me about the look on the little thief's panty-face in that split second when he heard the hammers fall on the primers, the split second before the glass shattered and he launched backwards through the door. I still didn't see blood.

Wesley thought he should talk for everybody. "They already took him to the hospital. I'm giving her a ride over there right now."

"He was still alive?" I said. I couldn't imagine anyone surviving the shotgun.

Wesley shot me that look again, like I had something to do with the story, like I was a suspect.

"Barely," Zona whispered.

"But I don't see how," I said. "Both barrels. He had the triggers set up."

Wesley leaned down in my face, but I didn't back away any. I had won nearly fifty bucks on a horse race a half hour ago. The money had gone straight to my backbone. "What the hell are you talking about?" he asked.

"The shelf." I leaned my bike against a pump (which was still on) and walked toward the taped-off door. Wesley didn't stop me. Instead, he followed, even lifted up the tape for us. Cigarette cartons lay scattered across the floor. The door that led to the garage was open, and I smelled old oil and grease. When I ducked down, I could see the shotgun still in its hidden place. I pointed where I looked and stepped out of the way. Wesley bent down and stuck his eyes close to the glass. He recoiled like he'd seen a snake. "Damn," he said. He walked behind the open register, reached down and pulled out the gun.

He broke the breech and showed it to me. The chambers were empty. Mr. McGill had put an empty gun in his secret shelf.

On the ride home, I wondered about people who did things halfway. Mr. McGill had gone to all that trouble to build a hiding place and take a hacksaw to his old 16 gauge, and in the end, he couldn't bring himself to slide a couple of shells in the chamber, couldn't convince himself to pull the trigger and cut a tiny robber in half. He knew the guy with the panty over his face would come back. He'd been sure of it. Mr. McGill just couldn't pull off the complete surprise.

When my mother walked in from her shift at the hospital, I waited for her in the kitchen. She told me as much of the story as she knew. Mr. McGill had a heart attack at some point during the third robbery. Nobody knew exactly when. He wasn't talking about it yet. And nobody knew how long he lay on the floor behind the counter once the little man took off. The tall wife found him there when he didn't stumble home an hour or so before dark.

That night, I sat on my bed counting my winnings again. I wondered what Mr. McGill thought about while he felt his heart giving out. What ran through his head? Did he think about luck? About the brand of fate that brings a man with panty hose stretched across his face back time and time and time again to the Esso station? Did he imagine what would become of his tall wife? Or if I'd remember to turn off his pumps? Did he think about longshots? Would he put any money on waking up alive tomorrow? Then again, I wasn't sure if Mr. McGill was a betting man.

WHAT IT MEANS
TO BE POOR

LATE ONE SPRING WHEN MY MOTHER GREW TIRED OF
shift work at the hospital, she took a job as a home health
nurse for Williamsburg County. This leveled a particular
burden on my father, who was forced to change the oil and
reset the points and have the tires balanced on the turquoise
Chevy Bel Air that my mother had brought to the marriage at
its beginning. "You'd think the county would provide a car for
their people," he said, annoyed at the extra tasks, but when
my mother reminded him that she would be paid mileage for
crisscrossing the county every day, he quieted down, no doubt
doing quiet math in his head, sums that would benefit him at the
close of every month. My mother saw this not only as a chance
to exercise her nursing skills in a new arena, but also as a way
to teach us—me and my brother—important lessons about
life in the world outside of our neighborhood. "I want you to
see how the other half lives," she said. And while I couldn't
do math in my head like my father, I'd learned enough about
ratios and proportions to know the world wasn't divided into

neat, perfect halves. I could tell she was convinced we would learn everything we needed to know about life from watching her perform the duties of a home health nurse. She couldn't even separate her own halves—the nurse and the mother. So she combined them a couple of days a week, when she picked us up from school in the Bel Air and made us climb into the wide back seat.

She'd crammed the front with cardboard boxes of brown pill bottles and a couple of ice chests she used to keep medicines cool in the sun. The Bel Air didn't possess air conditioning and the trunk had been permanently sealed since the morning my mother backed into a light pole in the IGA parking lot. Eli and I shared the back seat with a spare tire and a jack and a set of rusted jumper cables. She would point the Bel Air out of town, down roads I didn't recognize, directions I'd never imagined, but I could tell just from the trees and the dank smell of the air blowing through the open windows that we were headed toward the river, which led me to believe that the other half lived—for some reason—where it was wet and boggy. Eventually, she would pull up to a trailer balanced on cement blocks or a plank shack with sheets hung across the windows. Often, the doors and window frames of the shacks were painted a bright blue. When I asked my father about it, he said, "That's how those folks keep evil spirits away. Blue scares them off."

If there was a tree, she'd park the Bel Air in the patch of shade. If the yard where the shack or the trailer sat was bare, she'd remind us to keep a breeze on ourselves with the funeral home fans she handed out. One hot day, I'd had enough of the sweat and the mosquitoes that found their way into the car and said, "I can't see how the other half lives from inside the car, you know," and it was like I'd stuck her with a knitting needle. "You're right. Carry this box for me," and she herded me and my brother toward the front door of a house that canted to the left like it had being struck by a hard crosswind.

I saw a couple of dogs peering out from the dark under the porch. When we hit the steps, one of them let out a low growl. I saw Eli's eyes widen and he hooked a finger through a belt loop on my jeans. "Shut up, Truman," my mother hissed and the growl stopped. She even knew the names of their dogs. I wondered if that was what made her such a good nurse.

The door opened before she had a chance to knock and a woman the color of an old penny filled the space. "She ain't any better," the woman said and walked away, which I guessed was enough of an invitation to enter because we followed her right into her house.

"Burl, have you been giving her the medicine?" my mother asked. I'd never heard of a woman named Burl.

"These yours?" Burl asked back, pointing at us.

"When they act right, I claim them," my mother said and the woman smiled like my mother had just passed a test of some kind.

Inside, the house was as hot as the Bel Air. I saw an entrance into what I figured was a kitchen and on the other side of the room was a doorway to a bedroom. I saw a metal headboard strung with clothes. The house smelled like the dark odor of the swamp and the last meal that had been cooked—greens or fish, maybe. In the room where we stood was a couch that had once been covered with flowers and vines, but the pattern had all but faded into a single solid, bland color. A couple of wooden chairs flanked the couch and on a packing crate, a tiny black and white television was on but silent. I recognized the show. It was what the Charleston station ran in the afternoons for kids just out of school. *The Happy Raine Show*, with this white woman trying to act like an Indian. She told stories before the cartoons played. My father said her real name was Loraine and she wasn't any more an Indian than he was. *So the other half watches the same TV shows that me and Eli do*, I thought. That seemed more than fair.

Perched on the couch was a little girl with eyes too big for her head. The thin hair on her head stood up like the fuzz on a baby bird. She pulled her knees up to her chin and wrapped herself up with arms the size of rope. Her skin shone with the same color as her mother's, a dull copper. She squirmed on the couch, shifting herself back and forth. That was when I remembered my father talking about people who lived out in Sandy Bay swamp. He called them brass ankles. "They are all mixed together, a little Indian, a little white, a little bit of black. Comes out as brass ankles," he said like he was reporting the news on television.

My mother sat on the couch and nodded us toward the two wooden chairs. She cut her eyes at me and I knew what she was saying behind her expression: *You wanted to come inside and see. Well, careful what you ask for, smart aleck.* I thought I saw something move below my feet and I jerked my knees up. Under my chair, the floorboards separated enough that I saw dogs shifting beneath us, looking for cooler places in the crawlspace. In all that heat, right at that moment, I thought about winter and the cold air that would flow through those cracks in the floor.

My mother cupped the little girl's face in her hands. "Tasha, have you been taking your dessert?" she said. At the sound of the word *dessert*, Tasha rolled her face into a grimace and squeezed shut her gigantic eyes.

"Doesn't matter what you call that stuff, it still tastes like cat piss," Burl said. My mother ignored her and told me to run out to the car and grab the smallest cooler, the one marked PW. I wanted her to assure me Truman wasn't going to come into the sun and check me out, but my mother had already turned back to the little girl, rubbing her head and telling her that she was going to have dessert early today.

I found the cooler in the front floorboard and opened it. Inside were a dozen brown bottles all the same size, all with the exact same label: *Pin worm treatment—two tablespoons twice a week for two weeks—then recheck.* I'd heard of people getting worms before, always poor people who too often kept their hands in their mouths, but I'd never actually seen somebody who had stuff like that living inside them.

I handed the cooler to my mother and she pulled out a bottle of syrup. She already had a spoon in her hand. The little girl's eyes grew wider when she saw the brackish colored medicine thread into the spoon, and she began to hum low in her throat, almost like the growl that came out of Truman. "Now, Tasha, remember your prize," my mother said and tapped a sucker I hadn't noticed, stuck in the front pocket of her nurse's tunic. Tasha was on my mother's lap now, and she'd wrapped Tasha in a sort of gentle wrestler's hold, pinning down the little girl's stick-thin arms that wanted badly to flail. My mother pried open Tasha's lips with the leading edge of the spoon, and I saw dark spaces where teeth were supposed to be. Eli couldn't decide which was more interesting—the cartoon on *The Happy Raine Show* or the drama behind him on the couch— so his head swiveled back and forth. The hum coming out of Tasha tuned up higher and higher until it became a full-fledged shriek, so loud I didn't notice somebody walk in from the back door of the house, didn't notice Darlene McKenzie make her entrance, Darlene McKenzie who was in my class at school, the girl everybody feared and everybody avoided because she was big and strong and didn't care about much of anything. Once, she had pulled a fistful of a girl's hair right out of her head during a fight in South Carolina history class. She saw me immediately. But she never stopped walking, just made a steady, straight line through the room and when she passed me, I looked away, toward the television, so I didn't see the elbow she threw. It caught me on the shoulder and knocked me off the wooden chair. When I hit the floor, I was staring right through one of those spaces, looking Truman right in his yellow eyes.

LATER, ON THE ride out of the swamp and back to town, I thought I had discovered a rare fact about the other half and how they live. One of their members can knock you off your feet and the cartoon on the TV is still more interesting. My mother didn't seem to care I was on the floor. The only thing she said in the living room was, "Is she in your class?" The appearance of Darlene quieted her little sister, probably, I assumed, because Tasha had been on the receiving end of Darlene's elbows in the past. Nobody apologized or helped me up. Truman tried to lick my face through the floorboards. On the ride home, my mother did ask me to consider how to act at school the next day. "That girl—what is her name?—is probably embarrassed that you saw the inside of her house. From what I could tell, she has a great deal of pride." My mother sounded like she was a fan of Darlene's. I wasn't completely sure how pride was synonymous with a cheap shot from an elbow. Maybe that was another tactic the other half employed to keep my kind off balance. "Just be a little gentle with her," she said.

But Darlene was not gentle with me the next morning. She pinned me between two sets of green lockers just off the science hall. She was a good half a foot taller than I was—and I was tall for my age. She leaned into me and I smelled the inside of her house on her breath. "You shouldn't have come there," she said. Darlene's face was round and copper-colored, her dark eyes set back under her forehead. The arm she used to pin me in the space between the lockers was covered with dark hair. The thing I remember most is that her teeth were white and almost perfect, as if she'd had braces. She ought to try smiling more, I thought. "I don't want anyone knowing where I live. I don't want anyone knowing anything about me. You understand?" I started to answer but before anything came out of my mouth, I saw Darlene wince like a little electric shock had just run through her. Her eyes narrowed and she bit down on her jaw. She kept the one arm across my chest, but she reached around her with the other and I could tell she wasn't thinking straight when she scratched her rear end. Then, she remembered what she was doing and pulled her hand away. "Dammit," she said, releasing the pressure on my chest and walking off.

I had two classes with Darlene McKenzie that day and I watched her closely, watched her from the corner of my eyes so she wouldn't know. She never sat completely still, squirming and weaving in her desk the same way her little sister had on the couch that afternoon. That same wince flashed across her eyes. By the end of social studies, I was pretty convinced Darlene McKenzie had worms.

IT WASN'T HARD to steal the bottle. In the evening, when my mother returned from the road, she would bring the coolers inside our house and store all the medicines in the refrigerator for the night. Then she usually made herself a Tang and Smirnoff and put her feet up on the coffee table in the living room. She liked to sip her drink there in the dark, where no one else ever really sat. If my father was around, she'd send him to the Bantam Chef for a bucket of chicken or a bag of cheeseburgers. After a couple of drinks, she would shuffle upstairs in her nurse's uniform and watch TV in her bedroom until she fell asleep.

All I had to do was wait until I heard the television sound disappear and sneak downstairs to the kitchen. I had studied Darlene for a couple of days, and I was sure about the worms, and I was positive she wouldn't do anything about it, wouldn't take care of herself. She would never own up to something that weak and private. I hit the bottom step and weaved through the dark into the kitchen and pulled the handle of the fridge. The light and cool air spilled out, and I grabbed a bottle of worm medicine that looked about half full. I held it up and studied it in the light. I figured that would be enough doses to help Darlene. Behind me, in the shadows, my father said,

"Cough syrup or pin worm medicine?" I lost my grip on the bottle and it rattled to the floor but didn't break.

My breath was coming too fast. "I'm just thirsty," I said.

"Me too," my father said, from his seat. My eyes adjusted some. I could make out a can of Old Milwaukee. "Actually, I was hungry." With his half a stomach, my father never really ate food. He mostly drank things. His meals ran the gamut from turkey gravy to Old Milwaukee, but almost always liquids. "So, you must have worms since I haven't heard you cough," he said. "Lucky we have a nurse in the family."

I still held the bottle in my hand. "I don't have worms," I said and he cocked his head, waiting for more. "This isn't for me." When I thought back on it later, that was the moment I could have put the bottle back on the shelf. The door was still open, the light still streaming out. But I didn't. It never crossed my mind to go backwards then.

"You think your mother won't miss a bottle of medicine? You may think she doesn't keep track of things, but she does. Carefully," he said and took a sip from his beer. "I ought to know."

"I'm thinking about telling her later, after," I said. "She'll understand when I tell her what it's all about."

"And you're not telling me, right?" he said.

"It's for the other half," I said, knowing that would confuse him a little. I wasn't wrong.

"Goodnight," he said. "Your worm secret is safe with me. I feel for you. I know parasites." I shut the door and left him sitting in the dark, again.

The next morning, I tucked the bottle in my book bag and headed off to school. Darlene and I had PE together second period. Coach Reynolds had given up trying up trying to teach the boys soccer, so he blended the classes together. Now we played dodgeball with the girls who were easy targets, all except Darlene. She threw like a quarterback. She'd made two boys bleed on the same day.

I hadn't really rehearsed what I was going to say to her, how I was going to explain that I suspected she had worms, and I possessed the cure in a little brown bottle. Probably because there was no way to predict Darlene, no way to guess how she would react. I knew I had to tiptoe into it. Or maybe not. Maybe just come right out and say it. And I wasn't quite sure *why* I was trying to help her out. We would never be friends, more than likely never see each other after middle school. Darlene had already announced that when the eighth grade was over, she was getting a job and leaving town. One of the two was true. She would quit, but nobody like Darlene ever really left town. You could see all the other Darlenes on Saturdays, walking around the front of the train depot downtown, still planning their big escapes.

We changed into our PE uniforms, the faded gym shorts and blue t-shirts and made our way toward the gym. The girls dressed in a locker room on the other side of the basketball court. Darlene's shorts were always too small for her, riding high on her legs. Instead of heading to the middle of the court like usual, I weaved through my friends and intercepted Darlene near the baseline, under the basket. The brown bottle was tucked in the waistband of my shorts, under my shirt. I asked her to follow me.

Darlene tugged at her too-short shorts while we walked behind the bleachers. Nobody had really noticed us, which was good. "What?" she said. She backed up to a row of bleachers and rubbed against it. From a distance it might have looked like she was scratching her back, but I knew better.

"Listen, I know," I said, nodding toward her stomach. She raised her thick eyebrows, but stayed silent, so I repeated myself. "I know."

"What the fuck are you talking about?" she said. Very few people in school used that word. My father used it when he talked about Vietnam and drank at the same time. *Fucking Cong*, he would slur.

"I brought something for you," I said and lifted my shirt to grab the bottle. My stomach looked so white, especially standing so close to Darlene's copper skin. I held it out to her, like a birthday present or something. She leaned down and peered at the label. The next move was going to be hers. She moved her lips as she read. *Pin worm treatment—two tablespoons twice a week for two weeks—then recheck.* I waited for her forearm to come crashing down, for her to pin me against the stands. But she didn't do anything but sigh, and there, in her eyes, I saw Darlene panic. Then, she began to cry.

That was when I realized that a crying female is my weakness. In the many years since, I have gone to great extremes to keep women from crying. I have given them money, promised them jewelry. I have disappeared for good, just to prevent crying. But on that morning, in the blind spot near the backside of the bleachers, I had nothing to offer except a brown bottle of worm medicine. Plus, seeing tears come out of Darlene McKenzie was like watching a rare phenomenon, like a tornado slinging a cow through the air. It wasn't natural. She wasn't supposed to possess tears, but there they were welling up until her eyes could no longer contain them, dripping off her big, square jaw onto her PE t-shirt.

"It's no big deal," I said. "I won't tell anyone. Swear." Her eyes turned hard again, as if she remembered she had something to hate and that something was me.

"You'd better not," she hissed at me, glancing behind her. "And I ain't drinking that stuff. That's for babies. Babies like Tasha."

"You have to," I told her. "If you don't—" and I stopped because I didn't know what happened if you just never got rid of worms, never received any kind of treatment. My mother had never mentioned that.

"You can't make me," she said and started to walk away. I grabbed her by the arm and she spun back on me. "Why you doing this to me?" The tears, which had retreated, appeared again in her eyes. "You don't even know me."

It was a question I couldn't answer. When she walked into her house the afternoon I sat there, it was like a line—a line somebody had drawn in the sand when I wasn't looking—had been not only crossed, but erased. She'd seen something from my life, my mother and the way she wrestled with Tasha, and I had seen a big slice of hers—dogs in the crawl space, the smell of boiled collards that probably never went away. Maybe I didn't want that line to reappear. Maybe I wasn't comfortable with two halves in the world.

"Plus, that stuff tastes like shit," she said. "Tasha told me." I couldn't imagine Tasha using a word like that, and that was when I knew that Darlene had sampled the medicine at some point. Just a fingertip's worth, I guessed. Not enough to make a difference.

"It's not so bad," I said and I screwed the top off the bottle.

I smelled it immediately, like a mixture between sewer gas and rotting roadkill. I took a breath and tipped the bottle up, letting a good tablespoon drain into my mouth. When the worm medicine hit my tongue, my first impulse was to spit it back out, under the stands, but I held it in and swallowed. Darlene's eyes quit watering and grew bigger. I was sure I had impressed her somehow. I had stopped the crying. It had been worth it. Then I realized the surprise on her face was not anything I had done, rather Coach Reynolds hulking behind me, in the shadow of the stands. I felt his rough hand on my neck, and the only thing he said was, "Darlene, get your tail in line," and she ran toward center court.

MR. PATRICK DIDN'T really like the students at his school. Or rather, he didn't like dealing with their problems. When he stalked down the halls or around the grounds, the expression on his face wasn't what you'd expect from a principal. He seemed more confused and scared than mean, like he was trying to say, *I'm in a crazy mood. Don't make it worse.* The closest I'd been to his office was the wooden bench in the waiting area. The inside was a place reserved for, well, the likes of Darlene McKenzie. For the other half.

Coach Reynolds steered me out of the gym and down a couple of hallways, his hand never leaving the back of my neck. The only thing he said during the entire trip to Mr. Patrick's office was, "What's in the bottle, son? It says worm medicine but I don't buy that." I wasn't sure if he meant he didn't believe the label or he had never purchased the stuff. All I could manage to do was choke out the word *medicine*. I was too scared to make whole sentences. I'd heard stories about Mr. Patrick's, about what went on inside. The paddlings, the pain. My stomach ached with fear or perhaps because of the dose of rancid worm treatment. Coach Reynolds left me in the outer office, with the school secretary, and walked into Mr. Patrick's room without knocking. A few seconds later, Mr. Patrick appeared at the door and motioned me in.

His office was dark, the walls paneled with wood that was almost blood colored. Two lamps on either side of his desk were lit and glowing, the only things giving off any light. The blinds looked like they had never been opened to the outside. A small straight-back chair faced his desk, and he motioned me into it. My feet sank a bit into the thick carpet on the floor. The room smelled like cologne and fear.

I waited for Mr. Patrick to begin. I wanted him to cut into the silence. I thought he might yell at me. Instead, what came out of his mouth was quiet and measured.

"I don't want to embarrass you," he said. "Truly."

He paused like I was supposed to say something in return, but I was stumped and panicking. "You have two lamps," I said, as if I had witnessed a miracle.

"Yes, I do. But I want to talk about this," he said, holding up the bottle of worm medicine. "I know your mother is a nurse, son, and I know that if you had a problem she would be giving you medicine at home. So why are you drinking it at school? Coach Reynolds saw you."

I felt the words forming in my stomach, not far from where the ache had settled, the words that would explain the whole thing, how I had seen Darlene McKenzie's house and how she had pushed me into the lockers, so I wouldn't tell anyone about the dogs under the floorboards. Words that would explain how I watched her squirming in class, reaching behind her to scratch an itch that never completely went away. About stealing the bottle and that the only reason I drank it was to convince her that it didn't taste all that bad. The words formed like a burp in my throat now and all I had to do was open my mouth, just part my teeth and I'd be back in PE in about two minutes and Coach Reynolds would like me again, and the person they pulled out of line would be Darlene. They would probably send her to the school nurse, and before class was over, everyone would know that the big McKenzie girl was full of pin worms.

But I choked the burp back down, and when it finally returned, all I said was, "My momma doesn't know about my worms. I'm embarrassed to tell her. Nobody in my family has ever had anything like that." I lowered my head for effect. I felt Mr. Patrick's hand pat the top of it. It wasn't a gentle or compassionate touch, more like I was a family pet that had brought back the right bone.

Mr. Patrick walked to the door and I heard him ask the school secretary to call my mother. "She's already left the house," I said. "She works."

"We'll give it a try anyway," he said, his voice still syrupy. "We need to let her know about the medicine."

It turned out, my mother had not left the house yet. She was still packing up medicine, wondering how she'd miscounted her bottles the night before. In fact, when she walked into Mr. Patrick's office, she was actually a little happy that one of the tiny mysteries in her life had been solved. "So I'm *not* going crazy," she said. "*You've* got it." She glanced at me like we were strangers, and I could see her trying to connect the dots in the room.

Mr. Patrick sent me out into the outer office where I sat on that wooden bench, staring at the floor tiles, trying to decipher the mumbles I heard behind the thick door. My mother seemed to be carrying most of the conversation. I wondered how I'd be punished, figured now that I was safely outside of Mr. Patrick's office, a paddling was off the table.

The door swung open and my mother walked out with the medicine bottle in her hand. She thanked Mr. Patrick without looking back and grabbed me by the shoulder. "I'm taking you home," she said. "You know, what with your condition and all." She rolled her eyes so only I could see. She didn't say another word until we pulled up at the house and I laid my book bag on the kitchen table. The coolers were there, packed and ready for a day out in the county. I sat down as far away from her as I could.

"You do not have worms. If you had worms, you wouldn't be able to sit still and you'd wake up in the middle of the night crying because of an itch in crevices where you don't want to have an itch," she said. "Jesus. Ellis Patrick suggesting that I can't keep a close enough eye on my kids." She sighed and opened the cooler full of worm medicine and replaced the bottle I'd stolen.

"I'm sorry," I said.

"For what? Tell me what you're apologizing for and then we can talk." The pitch of her voice tightened. "I mean, were you showing off? Was it a dare? Were you trying to impress Darlene McKenzie or something?" Then, the switch flipped when she said Darlene's name, like the lights had suddenly come on in a room that had been dark since the moment she received the call from the school. She looked at me and I knew that she knew. My mother let out a long breath and settled into the chair beside me. She shook her head.

"You aren't going to tell me are you," she said, "even if I've figured it out on my own, right?"

I wanted to. For the second time that morning, I wanted to open up my mouth and set free the story. "I can't," I said. "Just can't." And I could have blamed my mother right then, told her that taking me out into the swamp to see how the other half lived started the whole thing.

She reached over and patted me on the head, the second time in an hour that an adult had done that to me. This one was different, though. This touch was light, just a feathery brush of her hand. "You're going to stay here at home for today. Maybe tomorrow too. I'll think about that," she said. She told me that her last call that day would be at the McKenzie's house. "I don't think you should come with me," she said. I thought about the size of Darlene's forearm, about the hair on it. "Help me carry these out to the car," she said.

I took the larger of the coolers and followed her through the house. She talked over her shoulder. "You know one of the things they teach you in nursing school?" she said, but didn't wait for an answer. "They teach you how to take care of people, sure, but the big thing is—and most people don't know this—they teach you how to get people to do things they don't want to do." She opened the back door of the Bel Air. "Almost like hypnotizing people. Do you understand?"

I handed her my cooler. She went on. "Listen, I can get people to swallow medicine that tastes like toilet water and smile about it. That girl won't even know how I found out she's had worms for the last month. She'll never know I found out from you. Promise." My mother made a little cross on her white uniform, just over her heart.

"She'll kill me," I said.

"She doesn't kill people," my mother said. "She just makes a lot of noise. Stop worrying. Women don't normally kill men. They just make them think they will. You're a good boy."

She eased the Bel Air out of the driveway, and I stood in the thick exhaust that settled in the morning heat. Maybe it was breathing in those fumes and having a dose of worm medicine in my stomach, but I suddenly knew I was going to be sick. Maybe it was fear. But I was supposed to feel better, safer. I was supposed to feel good about myself. My mother was going to make somebody well because of what I'd done. When I headed toward a shrub so I could throw up behind it, I could only think about the next time I saw Darlene McKenzie, how I'd look at her and wonder how mad she was about somebody coming into her house, somebody from the other half.

JOY TO THE WORLD

WE GOT THIS PART SECOND-HAND: THAT LAURICE REEVES
sat in the back seat of her father's Chevy Impala—the cream
one with thick white walls and tan interior—singing along
to the radio, singing loud because of the open windows, and
Hinson, her daddy, driving fast enough that the air flowed
through the car like a warm hurricane. Maybe Hinson told
her to be quiet, that he couldn't hear the real song, but Laurice
kept on singing because that's the way she was. She hated
being told what to do. Laurice had a temper and she came by
it honestly.

Seven years old, the Impala was beginning to show its age.
A tiny crack had opened up in the dash on the passenger side.
The lighter wouldn't light. And the glove box stuck unless you
banged it just right with the heel of your hand. The air conditioner worked but Hinson didn't much like the smell of fake
air. He suspected it might be unhealthy. So the windows were
open, even though it was the afternoon of July Fourth.

Hinson and Laurice drove toward the river, to Scout Cabin,
to set up for the fireworks show that evening. Every summer

Hinson volunteered to launch the show from the beach in front of the cabin. He knew to point the fireworks upriver and a little over the swamp. Even in the driest July, the swamp was boggy with wet pluff mud and smelly water, so there was never a danger of a fire if his aim was true. Even so, one of the pumper trucks always showed up, mostly to wind its siren at the beginning and end of the show.

Hinson always paid for everything, for all the fireworks. He hated the Chinese, he told us, because of some unspoken, personal occurrence during the Korean War, so he tried as best he could to buy stuff made in the USA, but it was next to impossible. Everything loud came from China—even Dixie Boy firecrackers were made in Macau. Sometimes, Hinson would jump around because he found a case of streamers from that English company, Pain's, at a stand in Myrtle Beach. Or he'd order buzz bombs from Standard's in India in March, so he'd be sure and have them by the Fourth. And it wasn't just the fancy airborne fireworks Hinson bought. He'd fill a second crate with Black Cats and Cobra Snakes and M-80s that he'd hand out like candy to teenagers whose parents let them play with explosive things. So they wouldn't feel left out, he brought sparklers for the little kids, as long as they were white. Hinson had never charged anyone for anything through the years—no tickets, no admission—but everyone knew his Fourth of July was a closed affair, that if you were black, the best you could do was watch a few dull flashes and hear the faint pops from the other side of town. Hinson only lit up the sky for white people on Independence Day.

That afternoon, Laurice rode, singing, stuffed between the two crates. Maybe she was thinking about the fireworks show that night, the way charred bits of paper the size of snow-flakes—the remnants of the Astro Fortune Cones and Star Glitters—floated down Black River for a good ten minutes after the siren sounded. Or the way her daddy's show lit up the bone-white beach at night. She probably wasn't thinking about the heat outside or the way the wind through the windows was beginning to feel hotter and hotter. Or the bend in the road to Scout Cabin that her Daddy had to brake for.

Sometimes things, people told us later, have to be just right to go *that* wrong. The slowing down for the curve. The cigarette lighter that wouldn't light. Hinson tamped a Marlboro from his hard-pack and tossed it on the seat. With both hands close on the wheel, he tore a paper match from a book and struck it. Then he probably remembered how stupid it would be to smoke with an entire fireworks show piled in the back seat. So perhaps he laughed and fanned the match and tossed it out the window. In that little bit of blowing space, the match caught some unfortunate wind, flared into flame again, then blew through the back window, landing in one of the crates.

I don't know if Laurice had a second to connect the dots, to realize amid the rush of wind and the whine of the radio, what a lit match might do in the big wooden crate of fireworks. I feel better thinking she saw nothing out of the ordinary, only heard what sounded like sudden drums beating out time that didn't match the song until the world around her exploded.

But we'll never know, because we got all this second-hand, because Laurice remembers next to nothing, because her daddy doesn't talk about it much, except on the weekends, when he drinks.

MY MOTHER FORCED me to visit Laurice in the hospital because that's where my mother worked. She was on duty the afternoon the ambulance brought her in. She was surprised Laurice wasn't burned more. "I think Hinson had more burns on him than Laurice," Mom said.

Laurice was hurt places other than the surface of her skin. Slow trails of blood dripped from both her ears. My mother said her eyes were wide open and unblinking, "like she'd just had the biggest surprise of her life," she said. And her mouth was open too, an interrupted mid-scream. "I don't mean to be flip," my mother said, "but your little friend looked like a cartoon that just stopped all of the sudden."

The people in the emergency room figured Hinson drove the car off the road into the bog, snatched his daughter from the deafening midst of the unexpected fireworks show in his back seat and tossed her into the brown, shallow water. They had to peel her out of wet clothes that smelled rank and decayed, like the swamp. But despite the fact he grabbed her as quick as he could, damage had been done. Both Laurice's eardrums were shredded by the noise and eventually Hinson lost an eye from a bottle rocket that launched at close range.

Hinson went home after a couple of nights, but Laurice stayed in the hospital waiting for her eardrums to scar over, waiting to see what would happen to her hearing. That's why my mother made me visit. "I see that poor girl watching the door every day. She doesn't get visitors much. Her daddy's almost embarrassed to show up," she said.

I have, from a young age, disliked hospitals. There are a handful of reasons, the most important being: I am uncomfortable with unexpected misery. Every time I walk into a hospital, I see some new form of torment inflicted upon a human being, a sight for which I am always unprepared. An odd half-limb or misplacement of facial features, even perhaps a unique sound of agony from behind a closed door. I am not comfortable with the surprises of suffering.

This, of course, I have come to realize over the years. Back then, I just knew I didn't want to see a girl whose head had been stuck in the loud, fiery core of a fireworks show, a girl who had to be dunked in swamp water to save. But my mother was a nurse, which meant she had a knack for convincing people to do uncomfortable things, so I followed her to the second floor of Kelly Memorial one afternoon and walked into Laurice's room.

I expected tubes and machines, but there she sat, not hooked to anything, cocking her head at me like a dog searching for a train whistle. Tiny red and black pock marks dotted her face and neck and arms. The marks weren't uniform, the largest the size of a quarter, and they glistened like they'd been dabbed with a clear, oily cream. Here and there, a Band-Aid appeared, but I wasn't sure what they were covering. Her left eye drooped half-closed as though she were tired on one side of her face. She smiled, happy to see me and that made me feel better. I didn't realize how unimportant my feelings were at that moment. Laurice screamed "HEY!" at me. My mother had filled me in about her hearing, the fact she couldn't pick up much of anything, but that it seemed to be slowly returning. For a while, though, she would be all but deaf. I expected the mottled, blunt speech the hard of hearing use. But Laurice was clear as a bell. Just really, really loud.

She yelled that she was going home in a couple of days, and that she was sick of eating Jell-O. She hollered that she didn't remember the fireworks going off in the back of the car. She screamed that the last thing she remembered was the song on the radio before all the noise and heat and color crashed in on her. It was "Joy to the World," by Three Dog Night. "ISN'T THAT FUNNY?" she yelled. "JOY TO THE WORLD."

We kept trying to give Laurice signals that she was plenty loud enough, but nothing worked. She kept on. My mother closed the door. She'd brought a little pad of paper with her, and she dug a pen from the pocket of her nurse's uniform. She wrote down: *Hon, we hear you fine*, and Laurice screamed, "THAT'S GOOD."

My mother whispered to me, "I don't think she's had anybody to talk to much." She wrote a note: *Where is your mother?* And Laurice hollered, "I THINK SHE WENT TO HAVE A CIGARETTE." My mother made a little growl in her throat. "You think they'd give up smoking after what happened," she whispered behind her hand.

Maybe it was unfair to talk about Laurice's parents right in front of her. She was suddenly from another country and didn't speak our language, and all she wanted to do, I could tell, was make some noise. I thought about borrowing the pad from my mother and writing questions to Laurice. Like, was she mad at her daddy? Or did she think she was going to die? Or what would she do if she was deaf forever?

But I didn't ask any of those. I just wrote down that I would see her later, when she got out of the hospital, which was true. I knew I'd see her riding her bike down my street. Or when my brother and I rode across Highway 52 to the Bantam Chef, I'd see her in the magnolia tree she always climbed. She would be different this time, though. She'd be the girl who got burned and couldn't hear us coming.

My mother's shift wasn't over for hours, so she walked me

down to the parking lot where I'd left my bike chained up. When she worked and my father was off on what my mother called one of his "tangents," my bike was how I got around town. On the way out, we passed the steel table where people sat and smoked. Hinson was the only one there, his Marlboro pack in front of him. He looked across the parking lot like he was trying to spot something way off in the distance. He didn't notice us standing there for a good two or three drags on his cigarette.

"Oh," he said, stubbing out the butt like a man caught doing something wrong. "I need to go back inside, I suppose."

I was glad my mother spoke. "Hinson, we're so sorry," she said. "Thank god nobody was hurt terribly. This could've been worse, trust me."

Hinson turned more toward us, so I could see the patch on his eye from a new angle. It wasn't pirate-like or sinister, like the ones in movies. It was more sad, like the fingerprint of a mistake. Made of gauze and tape, everything was held in place with a thick rubber band.

Hinson turned back toward the parking lot. "Worse?" he said. "I got one eye and poor Laurice is deaf as a stump. Tell me what's worse." My mother patted him on the shoulder, and he shrunk away like an animal scared of a new beating.

"At least y'all are still here. That's a blessing," she said.

Hinson dug into the Marlboros for a new one. He tore the top of the soft pack. "Blessings," he repeated. Now, I realize the expression on his face. Hinson was a man looking for somebody to be mad at, somebody to blame. But everybody was being so nice to him, he couldn't reach that place where he blamed himself, no matter how hard he tried.

LAURICE KEPT TO herself the rest of the summer. Even after her week in the hospital, she never showed up much on our street, just an occasional glimpse of her taking the corner fast on her bike. My mother said she heard Laurice's eardrums were better, but she would always be hard of hearing, that she would miss some of what was going on around her, "which may not be such a terrible thing," my father added. He was home and sour about the world in general because the upcoming school year was going to be different. It was the first year they were going to mix us all up. Black kids were coming from Cades and St. Stephen. We'd heard I would be having some black teachers, which scared me a little, but also gave me a chill of excitement. At that point in my life, a black person had never told me what to do, never graded me on anything. My father dreaded the school year, not because he had anything against black people. He just hated change of any kind on general principle. Change caused his repaired, half-stomach to act up, which usually turned him belligerent and toward the door for another tangent away from us.

A new private school in town was set to open in the fall, too, so a lot was going on, lots of people shuffling and resettling and fleeing in general. It wasn't so hard for us to decide what to do. With my mom's nurse salary (the only decent money coming in), my brother and I were, no doubt, going to the public school. I knew Laurice would be there too. Her daddy hadn't even replaced the Impala yet. Hinson still drove it around town, the interior smudged and charred, like a kind of badge of shame, or maybe just a reminder of how quickly things could blow up.

Like I suspected, Laurice was there on the first day of school, tanned, like she always seemed to be. All of us had parents dropping us off, just in case of trouble, but like most of the black-fears our parents had, they never amounted to much.

"Where's your momma and daddy?" I asked her. She cocked her head so I repeated myself louder. She got it.

"They wouldn't walk me, and I ain't riding in that car ever," she said. I noticed she wasn't as loud as she'd been in the hospital, but it was still too loud for school. She walked away like she'd said all she needed to, and I lost her among the bodies and heads roaming around, looking for room numbers and teachers' names—all the parents and their children, all the black and white heads. The whitest thing in the hallway was my mother's nurses uniform, and I was suddenly embarrassed. We stood out too much on a day when that wasn't a good thing.

My mother grabbed Eli by his hand and said she had to take him to his classroom. "You know where you have to go, right?" she said, but it really wasn't a question. She knew that even in the sixth grade, I—unlike my father— had no problem with change. I didn't want anybody holding my hand when I went to the classroom, number three twenty-six, that belonged to a Miss Frierson.

WHEN I WALKED into Miss Frierson's room, everything was quiet like church. All of the desks seemed to be filled by white kids and black kids, none of them talking, all of them staring in different directions. The room smelled of pine cleanser and mold. Rusty Thomasson peered out the window on the far side of the room, and there was an empty desk behind him. I headed for it. Miss Frierson was the blackest woman I had ever seen, her skin so dark that all the features on her face disappeared.

She wore sunglasses, so I couldn't tell if she was watching me or cutting her glance elsewhere. I walked by Laurice's desk on the back row, and she rolled her eyes at me. I was positive Miss Frierson could've seen her make that face, and for the first time that morning, a jolt of fear ran through me.

I only knew about half the people in the room. The other half were the new kids, black boys and girls I'd never seen before and a couple of underdressed country boys with skin rubbed red and raw from an unexpected cleaning. We were a roomful of sudden strangers. Rusty didn't say a word when I slid into the desk. Nobody knew the rules yet. Nobody knew which way Miss Frierson was looking.

For two or three minutes, we didn't challenge the silence in the room. We just stared. The shelves were neat with history and social studies texts, the walls bare of posters and charts. I thought I smelled a hint of new paint mixed in with the cleanser. Miss Frierson's desk was free of any clutter, just a big white Bible perched near her right hand, a coffee mug near the left. A bell finally sounded and we all jumped. A black boy near the radiator laughed, and Miss Frierson cut her sunglasses at him, shutting him off. She pulled a sheet of paper from somewhere—her lap or maybe a hidden pocket—and began to call the roll. Her voice was steady and a little higher pitched than I would have guessed. She barely moved her lips when she spoke, a thin slice of white teeth peering through the darkness of her face. The words floated over us without any emotion to carry them. She didn't look up from the paper, just made a mark with a pencil when we answered.

Laurice's last name was Reeves, so she was sort of near the end of the list. I'd kept my eyes on her after my name was called. Laurice had lost interest and began to doodle on the notebook in front of her. "Reeves," Miss Frierson all but whispered, and no one replied. Laurice rubbed her nose with the end of her pencil and went back to her sketch. "Reeves," she said again. "Reeves." From a distance, I tried to will Laurice to answer, but she was off somewhere, lost in whatever she was drawing. I raised my hand. Miss Frierson's head twitched slightly in my direction.

"Are you Reeves?" she asked.

"No, ma'am," I said. "I answered already."

"You may not go to the bathroom," she said, not more than a murmur.

"I don't have to go to the bathroom," I said. "Laurice didn't hear you."

"Who is Laurice?"

"Reeves," I said and pointed at the back of the room. The movement made Laurice look up. She shot me a wondering sort of expression.

Miss Frierson didn't say a word, just rose from behind her desk. She was a tall, thin woman, almost what you'd call bony. She walked toward Laurice, who still had no idea what was going on. Miss Frierson stopped over Laurice's desk. Her head seemed to be turned toward the window, as if she were staring at the playground. But we couldn't see her eyes.

"Why didn't you answer me?" she whispered out of the slit in her face.

Laurice looked from me up to Miss Frierson. Panic rushed behind her eyes when she realized that she'd missed out on something.

"Are you trying to show me up?" Miss Frierson said, and I finally made out some details on her face. The skin on her cheeks tightened up. Her voice quivered a bit. "Are you?"

Laurice did the worst thing she could've. She raised her hand and pointed to her ear. And she smiled. I knew Laurice, so I knew the smile meant to say she was sorry. Miss Frierson saw it different. She saw a white kid with a bone to pick on the first day of class.

"She can't hear you," I hollered, probably too loud. Miss Frierson spun on me.

"You, shut your mouth," she said quickly, the most energy she'd shown all morning.

"But she doesn't know what's going on," I said. "I mean, you got to at least speak up for her to hear you. She had an accident."

That's when Laurice reached up—while Miss Frierson looked in my direction—and touched her on the arm. Miss Frierson wasn't ready for that and she screamed. She ran to the door of the classroom and screamed again, this time calling what sounded like names into the hallway. Her shouts echoed and hung in the heavy air of the hall until two big white men ran in the room, took me and Laurice by the arm and steered us to the principal's office.

I DIDN'T THINK too much about it. Mr. Patrick, the principal, had a scared look on his face years before black teachers showed up at school, so it didn't surprise me that he'd do anything to avoid trouble so early this particular fall. He told us to just stay home until Monday. "You'll only miss a day," he said. "We won't call it a suspension. We'll call it a delayed beginning for you two." Mr. Patrick didn't want to start anything.

Which was fine by me. I didn't much care for school then, and I wasn't real sure I wanted to head back to a classroom run by a woman in sunglasses. I considered Mr. Patrick's proposal a gift. Laurice's dad didn't see it that way.

He arrived at school already mad, and even though it wasn't much after nine in the morning, I believe he'd been drinking something that fueled all the devils bothering him. He wore a higher quality patch on his eye now, a black one, and when he told the secretary behind the counter that the principal better "drag his ass out where I can see him good," he cocked his good eye at her like a gun.

Patrick stuck his head ground-hog-like from his office door, and Hinson charged behind the counter, waving his finger. "First day," he hollered, "first day and you got to pick on a pair a white kids."

Every time Patrick tried to answer or defend himself, Hinson cut him off with the finger or the patch. Laurice sat by me on a wooden bench. She leaned over and said too loud, "I can hear *him* okay," but nobody paid her any attention. Hinson appeared overly mad for what had happened in the classroom, like he'd flipped an on-switch and couldn't figure out how to turn it off.

"I want to see that teacher," he said, and it struck me funny, him wearing an eye patch and wanting to *see* all these things. Plus, Laurice being the cause of everything because she couldn't hear. The deaf and the blind, leading the way. It became too funny for me. I tried to keep from laughing but I couldn't. I clapped my hands over my mouth, but the sound burst through my fingers like escaping water. In a short pause in all the yelling, the only sound people heard was me, giggling like a crazy man, me trying to cram the laughter back into my mouth. Hinson turned on me.

"You think something's funny?" he hissed and I smelled his breath. This was bitter stuff, something close to flammable.

"Nossir," I said, but I couldn't stop laughing. He looked like a lost pirate, and his little girl with her pockmark scars and mostly-confused expression on her face was something I couldn't dodge. I glanced up at Mr. Patrick for help, but he had pulled his head back inside his office, probably happy I had somehow given him an escape route.

"This funny to you?" Hinson said, but before I could answer this time, he went on. "This is happening, you stupid kid. This is a real thing. And the last thing we going to do is laugh at it."

I had no idea what he was talking about, but there wasn't time for an explanation. The same two white men came in and told Hinson that he and Laurice better go. They laced their big arms across their chests.

While I waited for my mother, I found out the two men were coaches hired that year to teach P.E. and show us the sex-education movies and make sure the wrong kind of people didn't wander onto school property. They were new, but they were already good at their jobs.

THIS PART, I got first-hand, not because I wanted to, but because Laurice made me, really. She came by my house that next Sunday in the late afternoon, knocked on my door and yelled that I needed to follow her. Her bike leaned against the porch steps, and she'd been riding for a while because even through the screen door, I could tell her face was shiny with sweat.

"You got to see this," she hollered and jumped back on her bike. She was a half-block away before my feet found the pedals. She turned down the street that ran beside my house and dead-ended at the railroad tracks a quarter mile away. I kept her in sight enough to know that she was heading for the place we called The Dunes, a little strip of unused land between the end of the street and the elevated tracks, where the city dumped any of their spare construction dirt. We had big clay-colored hills to climb on all year long, hills close enough to the tracks that we could throw dirt clods at the trains passing above us.

Laurice rolled her bike into a hill of dirt and took off on foot for the tracks. When I wasn't breathing hard from chasing her, I could hear tiny, delicate *pops* in the distance, like far-off hunting rifles, some of them slightly louder than others. Laurice raced up the slope of gray rip-rap, slipping once on the rocks. She sprinted down the tracks a hundred yards, then came to a quick stop. She pointed ahead of her like an explorer sighting new territory, and when I reached her, the pops had turned into absolute roars of quick thunder. For a second, I thought I might be hearing the rumble of a train, but the tracks under my feet weren't vibrating. I looked down Laurice's arm, in the direction she pointed.

There, on the narrow, flat edge at the top of the slope sat Hinson, facing the other side of the tracks, his newest fireworks show lined up and sparking from the thin strip of railroad right-of-way, all of his noise and fire aimed at the small, wooden shacks that sat too close to the tracks down in Nicholtown. Like an artillery gunner, he adjusted the trajectory of the Roman candles so the trail of smoke streaked over the roofs. The bigger fireworks, the sky rockets and repeaters, normally aimed high over the swamp on the Fourth of July, exploded far below us, on the rooftops. From where we stood, we could see people, black people, scrambling ant-like for cover. Laurice covered her ears, her eyes wide. She became that cartoon again.

I took a step toward Hinson. I don't know why. I had no idea what I wanted to do. Maybe I just wanted a better look. Laurice pulled me back. She had reached her limit. She could go no closer to the sounds and to her father and didn't want me to leave her alone. She yelled at me, but it didn't matter what she said. I couldn't make out words among all the noise.

Then Hinson saw me and his daughter standing there. He stopped lighting fuses. The sun had dipped below the tree line, but there was still enough dusk to see Hinson's face, flickering in the flame from his lighter. The stink of burned gunpowder drifted over us in a heavy haze. The quiet fell down around us, and Hinson said, "I'm just trying to scare them. Not hurt them. That's all I want." He turned back to his lineup of rockets and paper cannons. Before he lit the next fuse, I heard a sheriff's siren somewhere in front of us, on the black side of the tracks, the wrong side if they wanted to catch Hinson and stop his fireworks show. When I turned to Laurice, she was just starting to cry, tears brimming her eyes. "Why did he say?" she asked, and she didn't yell at me. "What was it he said?" It was close to a whisper. But I heard her clearly. I remember wondering if I should lie or keep my mouth shut, so I did.

WHAT GETS TOSSED

1 The 4:15 from Georgetown—a long, messy train—stalled just as it was about to ease past my house, so Lonnie Tisdale and I had little trouble spotting the bright caboose through the trees. The small window at the top of the caboose was wide open, and not an engineer in sight. Lonnie and I walked to the tracks from my house, toward the dead end of my street where the county dumped sand and clay left over from road construction projects, perfect reddish hills like relatively fresh Indian mounds. We called them The Dunes. Most weekends we played army, hiding among them. But today, we decided to see if we could throw dirt clods into that open window of the caboose, because the train wasn't moving and we were unaccustomed with resisting temptation. I had a better arm than Lonnie. After a half dozen misses, I had zeroed in on the window and started chunking dirt bombs directly into the caboose. Lonnie giggled, said I was making a mess inside somebody's caboose. "But who rides on the back of the train anyway?" he asked.

2 We didn't hear the car pull behind us. We were too busy slinging dirt clods into a caboose, which is actually more fun than it sounds. Maybe Wesley the deputy had switched off the ignition and rolled to a quiet stop at the edge of the pavement. Lonnie happened to turn around for more ammunition and saw Wesley unfolding from his Sheriff's Department cruiser. Wesley was new on the force. His past was the latest mystery. The prevailing rumor was, he'd moved from Sumter, and nobody could understand why anybody with a future would leave Sumter for here. That wasn't even a lateral move, but maybe law enforcement drifted in unknown directions. He filled out his uniform like someone who used to like football. A cigarette dangled from Wesley's mouth, but it didn't make him seem any older or tougher. It just made him look like he'd come early to a Halloween party dressed like a policeman. He pointed at us and started winding his way among the mounds.

3 I should mention that during the previous school year, Coach Reynolds made a valiant attempt to teach all of the males in the seventh grade two things he felt would serve us well in the future: a working knowledge of soccer and an equally working knowledge of sex. He said soccer was the sporting wave of the future and sex was something that would eventually drive us crazy, no matter how much we studied it. Both of these subjects, which we tackled during PE class, did nothing but addle us. In fact, now that I think about it, that was a year of thick, unlifting fog and utter confusion.

4 Therefore, it should surprise no one that Lonnie Tisdale and I were still confused when summer arrived and the confusion gave way to boredom and our boredom gave way to throwing dirt through an open caboose window, and we ran from the large deputy policeman who snuck up on us. I don't remember whose idea it was to sprint. Maybe it was simply the fight-or-flight thing that kicked in. (When I say that, I realize I learned about fight-or-flight earlier that fall, in seventh grade biology, so something obviously stuck amid the confusion.) Lonnie and I took off down the railroad right-of-way, ripping through the briars and chokeberry volunteers that sprang high through the gray railroad rocks. We expected Wesley to yell at us to stop, to scream one of those official law enforcement orders like "halt" or "desist" or "stand down," but we couldn't hear much above the sound of our hard breathing as we stumbled over the loose rocks, finally reaching a place where a thin path opened into the woods on our right. We angled into the trees, and I glanced back when I thought it was safe. I saw Wesley behind us a couple hundred yards down the tracks, standing still, pointing at us with his finger like it was his toy gun.

5 During the last couple months of seventh grade Rachel McCutcheon moved to town. Her father was a big deal at the Drexel Plant. Drexel made the unvarnished furniture that shipped away each night on the 12:15am outbound train, the one that ran behind my house. Rachel sat in front of me during Miss Clara Wilson's South Carolina history class, and I studied the back of her blond head. One Tuesday, Miss Wilson drew forty-six lines on the board so we could fill in all blanks with our state's county names. That day, I remember Rachel McCutcheon wore a navy blue sleeveless shirt, and one blond hair—one renegade, perfect blond hair—was out of place, escaping across the freckled topography of her bare shoulder. I watched that hair like it was about to come to life and mock me. Neil Coker recalled that Newberry was a county and wrote it in a blank slot. Miss Wilson scanned the room, looking for another kid brave enough to trudge to the front of the class and write on the board. I glanced from the hair on Rachel McCutcheon's shoulder to the board and back again. I'd never been so hypnotized and so uncomfortable. Coach Reynolds had warned us about this kind of strange pain, back in the fall. In my head, I begged Clara Wilson not to call on me. I thought I might faint. Maybe she recognized the tight expression on my face. Maybe she saw the hair on Rachel's shoulder. She told Tony Cantey there was a county that began with the letter 'b' and that he should remember it because it was right down the road. I knew the answer. Berkeley. But I wasn't up to walking at that point in the morning.

 Wesley's cruiser idled in my front yard when Lonnie and I walked through the woods and back to my house. My father leaned against it, and I could tell that made Wesley nervous. The blue-and-white car was spotless and not to be touched. He had a beer in his hand—my father, not Wesley. Wesley drank iced tea from one of our Flintstone's jelly glasses. My father shook his head slowly when we walked up. There

was no sense running again, nowhere to run. "Wesley here tells me you been having some target practice with Southern Railway." He took the last sip of his Old Milwaukee and bent the can a little when he'd finished, a crinkly announcement that he needed a replacement. "I told him that you would clean up every bit of dirt in the caboose cab so—" Wesley cut him off. "But you can't be allowed inside the train. Railroad company orders," he said. My father didn't appreciate being interrupted. He scowled at Wesley. "I'm not a fan of having a police car in my yard. Makes the neighbors jumpy." Wesley decided that was his cue to leave because he reached in his pocket for the keys, then realized the car still hummed under the hood. "Since you can't really clean up, I'll let your daddy take care of the punishment," he said and ducked behind the wheel. "You boys are trouble." As the cruiser pulled out of sight, my father said, "If you're going to do something stupid like that, try not to get caught. Words to live by."

7 Lonnie stayed for supper because my mother didn't give him much choice. I'd had enough of him for the day. I blamed him for everything—for the caboose parking at the end of my road, for the open window, for the dirt, for our poorly considered escape. Dinner was quiet and nobody said anything about the cop in the yard until my mother piped up, "You need to take these boys to the woods," and I wasn't sure if that was her way of saying I needed a decent beating, which would, for some mysterious reason, have to take place among trees. My little brother kept his head down

and chewing because he had done nothing to be guilty for. "Take them camping. Get them away from town and talk to them about *things*." The last word rang like a dinner gong and the sound of it hung over the table. "I haven't camped since Dong Nai. I didn't much like it then. Doubt if I will now," my father said. He slurped broth along with a few spoonfuls of white gravy, the heaviest thing he could stomach with all of his digestive problems. "Anyway, I don't think I'll be around this weekend." My mother did not flinch or falter. "You will be camping this weekend. You will be with your son and his shiftless friend"—Lonnie smiled because he didn't grasp the definition of shiftless—"and you'll explain about law and order and men and boys and girls. Do you understand what I'm saying?" She fixed her stare on him. He looked down at his gravy as she continued. "And this isn't Vietnam. Don't drink from mud puddles this time," she said, "and you'll be just fine." She rose from the table and grabbed the phone from the wall. She stretched the cord into the kitchen for some privacy, but we could hear her explaining to Lonnie's mother that her son would be in the woods that weekend, learning things.

 One place in town sold records, the Rose's store on Main. Just inside the front door and to the right stood a few racks of LPs and several bins of 45s. You could flip through records and watch people pass on the sidewalk outside the big front window. I had some money left over from the Belmont Stakes bet I had won the day of Mr. McGill's heart attack. I bought the 45 of "Let It Be." My mother liked The Beatles but my dad

thought they were Satanic British emissaries come to under-
mine all he'd sacrificed in Vietnam. Instead of a Southeast
Asian parasite, he instead blamed the British Rock invasion
for his lack of a properly functioning stomach. The flipside of
"Let It Be" was "You Know My Name (Look Up the Number)"
but I didn't care about a B-side. I first picked up the song on
my little transistor radio, from WKSP, the tiny AM station
out on Sumter Highway. When I heard McCartney sing about
Mother Mary, I, for some reason, always thought of Rachel
McCutcheon, thought about how she would like it too, how
it would undoubtedly speak to both of us if we just had the
chance to listen together. I thought about that blonde hair. I
bought "Let It Be" on a Thursday after school and pedaled to
Rachel McCutcheon's house on the far side of town, one of
the good neighborhoods with hedges and fire hydrants. I took
the 45 out of the paper sack so she could see the actual sleeve
and the green apple on the record's label. In my head, I begged
for her to open the door and suddenly there she was. I had
surprised her, which I counted as a good thing. Her hair was
brushed smooth. I didn't even say hello. Instead, "I brought
this," I said, holding up the 45. "It's new. The Beatles." Her
nose turned up and I felt one knee give way. Man, that nose.
"I don't even like The Beatles," she said and half-slammed the
door without waiting to hear what I might have to say next. I
stood on the porch like an ornament for a few seconds, thinking the closed door was a joke I didn't get, but the knob never
turned again. On the way home, I pedaled to the railroad
tracks near The Dunes, slid the record out of its sleeve and
slung "Let It Be" like a flying saucer toward the gray rocks. I
heard it land badly.

9 We hiked maybe a couple of miles down a sand road—me, Lonnie Tisdale and my father. We followed my father because he seemed to have an idea where he was headed. The road sloped gently in the general direction of the river. The air we walked through was heavy, thick with humidity, and it smelled like the swamp always smelled, like something large and meaty had died and was in mid-rot, upwind. Each of us carried our own gear. My father insisted on that. "Never expect somebody to pick up your slack. Let's call that number one," he said. We soon realized he was numbering the lessons we would learn on the trip. For instance, after slogging along under our packs for half an hour, he turned back to us and said, "Walk in a straight line, boys. That way the curves won't bother you as much. That's numero tres." Lonnie whispered to me, wondering how many lessons we would get, all totaled. He wanted to lay a bet on a number. And I hadn't understood a single one of my father's lessons yet. They were mysteries I couldn't ask about. Like when we pounded tent stakes into the soft ground and my father yelled, "Always look where the hammer falls. Number sixteen!" We cooked hotdogs over red coals and listened to the tree frogs come out as the sun bled away into evening. "If you shit in the woods, stomp around before you squat. You don't want a water moccasin lighting you up," he said. "I will not number that one. That's just pure common sense." We stoked the fire with new wood and my father pulled a bottle from a small side pocket of his pack. The brown liquor shimmered behind the glass in the firelight. He took a long sip. "Tell me, boys," he said, "what's the stupid-est thing you've done lately?" He took another, smaller sip

and spit toward the fire. The flames flared like a magic show. "Other than throw dirt at trains, of course."

10 Lonnie didn't have to think long. "I stuck my tongue in the electric socket one night. I couldn't taste anything salty for a month." My father nodded at him, silently agreeing on that particular level of stupidity. I had a list to pick from. Like the neighborhood intersection I coasted through on my bike a dozen times with my eyes closed, just seeing if I could, until the afternoon a pick-up almost ran me over. Or the alligator I tried to jump one morning while he was sunning and asleep on a sandbar. Or the time I fell through the attic floor chasing a possum but didn't break anything important. But instead, what I said was, "I bought a girl something she didn't want." There, in front of the fire, I remembered how stupid I'd felt that afternoon, standing on Rachel McCutcheon's porch. I couldn't shake that feeling. "Now we're getting somewhere," my father said. "Heartbreak and disappointment. The dull ache of rejection. We know it all too well, don't we, men?" He sipped again, then held the bottle out to us. Lonnie shook his head but I decided to see what the story was with brown liquor, because I knew that there was, indeed, a story in that bottle. "Careful, Sparky," my father said. "Pace oneself." The bourbon sizzled on my tongue and somehow the smell and the taste and the heat flew through my nose to my eyes. I spit onto the fire before I choked and the flames jumped. Lonnie whistled and said, "Damn, that's cool," but my father wasn't impressed. He smiled, "Number twenty-two. Don't try new shit until you're good and ready for it."

11 My father waited until the fire burned down low enough we couldn't see each other's faces. I believe that was his signal to talk about subjects that could embarrass us, the topics Coach Reynolds might have ignored during the foggy season of soccer and sex education. My father proceeded to tell us about how he avoided the clap in Vietnam by pre-screening hookers, because, as he said, "I was lonely, boys, but loneliness should never cloud judgment. Number thirty." He explained the origin of babies, a process he called "the cruel bottom line of unbridled passion." He told us throwing dirt through an open caboose window was simply the first ripple in a set of criminal rings that would widen until one day we found ourselves in prison, fending off muscle-bound murderers who wanted to bugger us on a regular basis. We told him we had never heard the word "bugger" before. He was about to explain its meaning when a pair of car headlights ghosted through the trees. My father grabbed a plastic jug of drinking water and doused what remained of the dying coals. "Number thirty-six," he whispered. "Value invisibility."

12 A couple of weeks after I tossed "Let It Be" on the bank of railroad rocks, the Youth Center held its first Teen Canteen dance of the spring. Kids who were honest-to-god couples slow-danced to a high-pitched Michael Jackson song, and if they were the brave pairs, perhaps managed a modified, shuffling shag to some beach song about boardwalks and sand. The rest of us wandered the darker perimeters of the big, echoey room, hoping to look unaffected by our loneliness and uninterested in altering our situation. Lonnie and I walked outside, to the back of the cement block building and stared down the hill toward the baseball field, and just beyond that to the railroad tracks we couldn't see in the darkness but knew were there. I smelled mowed wild onions. A glow suddenly appeared in the dark just off our left and framed inside of it, I recognized the outline of Rachel McCutcheon's face. She blew a bored cloud into the dark. Lonnie lied about having to go to the bathroom and walked back inside just as Rachel took another drag. I had told him about Rachel McCutcheon's renegade blond hair. I had never seen anyone my age smoking a cigarette. My eyes adjusted to the dark. She held the cigarette loosely in her fingers, as if she'd been born with it there. "Why did you bring me that record?" she asked and I panicked to invent a quick answer that wouldn't make me sound like a kid on Santa's lap, doling out his wish list. "Because I thought you needed to hear it," I said finally, and she seemed to enjoy the simple answer, smiling as she rubbed the butt against the cement wall. "I lied," she said. "I really do like The Beatles, especially George." I heard a starting gun fire somewhere in my head, and I leaned toward her face, and when she didn't retreat, I put my mouth on hers and tasted smoke. I felt as though I had just walked into a strange room in a strange house and the door locked behind me. My eyes were still closed when Rachel McCutcheon slapped me, sending bright stars scorching across the blackness behind my eyes. But kissing her was not one of the stupidest things I'd ever done.

The sand road we had hiked in on resembled a levee, elevated a few feet higher than the beach, where we had pitched our tents at the river's edge. We sat stock-still and followed the headlights meandering down the road, until they eventually stopped where the sand ended, about fifty yards from our dead fire. The moon had risen by then, not full, but enough to shine a dull glow on the outline of the car, a big car, maybe a Buick or an Olds, the wrong kind of car to be in the swamp. My father punched me on the arm and whispered, "Follow me," and began low-walking slowly toward the car, Lonnie and I sneaking right behind. He stopped halfway to the car, pulled our heads close, and whispered his plan, his voice wound tight with excitement. He sounded like a little kid. He took on the hard part—commando crawling across the sand at the rear of the car to the other side of the levee, for a few seconds in clear view of whoever was inside. Lonnie and I crouched down, but we didn't need to. We could stand upright and our heads would still only rise to fender height. We both peered around the rear of the car and saw that my father had made it to the other side of the levee-road. I heard a metallic *ping* as the engine cooled down. The fender I touched with my palm was already cold in the damp air. We waited on my father's signal, but before it came, the dome light inside the car winked on. My breath caught bone-like in my throat and Lonnie took a step to run, but I snagged him by the shoulder. I glanced up and in the dull, yellow light, saw a guy above me, his bright Hawaiian shirt unbuttoned and open. He'd only cracked the door to spit into the dark. Beyond him, a woman with long hair unraveled herself from a white bra and

her breasts spilled into the glow, then disappeared quickly out of our view. The man hocked and spit again, something wet landing in the sand behind us. He slammed the door, and it cracked like a gunshot in the dark swamp. A long minute later, we heard the woman moaning. She was calling for Charles. The car—it was an Olds, I could see that now—began to rock on its shocks. I watched for my father. I saw him mouthing a count: *one, two, three*—and when he hit three, we banged on the fenders of the car with our open palms and yelled like our throats had been cut. We screamed until we were coughing and out of breath, then according to plan, sprinted to the edge of the dark, where we watched the panic play out inside the car. We saw arms and legs flailing with each other. The woman screamed a reply to us. He yelled as well, not at anybody in particular, just at the general darkness. A door opened and light flowed out. The woman tried to jump and run but he snatched her back inside. She glowed completely white for a couple of seconds. We heard the ignition fire up and the transmission slammed into reverse, fishtailing back the way it had come, the screams of the driver and passenger echoing over the roar of the big, throaty American engine.

14

The morning after Rachel McCutcheon's short, smoky kiss, I still sensed her sting on my cheek. I didn't mind. At least it was something I could grab hold of, so to speak. I had nothing to do that day, until my paper route in the afternoon, so I walked through the woods to the railroad tracks and tried to remember which direction I'd flung "Let It Be." I knew I had stopped near the end of the paved road, near where the county dumped the fake Indian mounds. I walked back and forth for twenty minutes, tacking like a bird dog in search of a scent. I finally spotted the black vinyl glistening in the sun. I was wrong. I had only imagined the record shattering on the rocks. In fact, only a single piece of vinyl was chipped away, a thin, cuticle-shaped sliver along the edge. The last three-quarters of the song would play just fine, I thought. I didn't notice until I got home that "Let It Be" had taken the direct hit. The song was way too scratched to play. But the flip side was fine. I decided to be happy with what I had.

15

We laughed until we fell asleep in the tent. The next morning Lonnie and I walked up to the road to check out the ruts the Olds left when it peeled away in the dark. Just at the border of the sand, I spotted a shoe, a fancy woman's shoe with a thin heel and a buckle, lying perfectly upright, as if someone had placed it gently in the sand, like it was waiting for the missing foot. I took the left shoe back to our tent. "She must've kicked it out when she was flopping around," Lonnie said. "She's going to miss that." My father called it a trophy. "Spoils of war, boys," he said. We packed our gear and leaned into the slope on the way to the road. My father asked us what we had learned in the woods. Neither of us answered for a few steps, until Lonnie finally said, "Don't go parking with a woman on a dead-end road." My father nodded. "Works for me. What about you?" he said. The way he asked, I knew he expected better from his

son, something more profound. I fingered the shoe still in my
hand. I thought for another second. My father stopped walking, so I did too. "Tell Mom what she needs to hear, tell her
you got us all straightened out," I said and threw the shoe as
far into the woods as I could. I never heard it land. "Good boy.
Let's call that number forty-one," he said like a man proud of
himself for something unexpected.

YOU DREAM,
YOU LEAVE

THE ONE THING FLIPPER ALWAYS TELLS US IS, IF HE EVER comes across any money, he'll hit the road and track down the mother of invention, and when he finds her, he's gonna scratch the bitch's eyes out and leave her tapping her way down the road with a short stick.

Whenever he says this, every one of us, including me, asks him why, though we know the answer. It's like a pretty good joke with a decent punch line we've heard a dozen times before. But we still have to play straight men for him. We have to lead him on.

"Because I been inventing ways to get by all my life. I'm tired of inventing. I'm wore slap out. You'll be too one day," he says, waving his beer can at us.

But we're all too young to be tired yet. Flipper's got a few years on us. He's seen more of the world. He was even in the Army for three months. The Army gave him a regulation hair-cut and fitted him up for his uniform, then Flipper broke his nose climbing across the monkey bar looking things, and the

165

Army let him go when he started having nose bleeds on a regular basis. He walked out of the gate with a clean pair of boots and two full uniforms. He still wears the faded green shirts, only he's cut the sleeves out. So his shoulders can get some sun, he tells us. His nosebleeds quit the minute he left Ft. Jackson, he says.

We're still young enough or stupid enough to dream we can get out of this place, or to think that something big might happen nearby to make staying here a little more worthwhile. I mean, all of us who sit at the station imagine ways to leave town. Some are real simple plans, like catching the bus out on Highway 52 for Florida, but to me, for some reason, that seems too easy. Any fool with an arm and a mouth can flag down a bus. My idea is that if you're leaving a place like Kingstree or any spot you're not particularly fond of, you got to go out big, so if you fall on your face somewhere and come running back with your tail tucked, at least you can brag about the figure you cut when you left.

So at nights, I lie awake in bed and dream up ways I might head out of town. In my favorite one, there's this woman in a white sports car who pulls into the station and says, "Anybody *here* know about these *here* kind of automobiles?" in a voice so smooth you could spread it on soft bread. Of course, since this is my dream, I know how to fix anything, so I crawl up under her car and bang on something, pretending like I'm tinkering, but I'm really looking below the chrome rocker panel at the bottom of her shins, wondering if she shaved her legs in a tub full of bubbles that morning.

By the end of this dream, she'll be the one I leave with. I try not to think too much about the end of the story. I try to stretch it out and make it last. I add things as I come by them, since there's no telling how long I could be at the station, no telling how long I'll be in this place.

In the meantime, back in the real world, we sit and watch Flipper drink beer. Drinking beer's how he was pegged with his nickname. Somebody in the Army found out that when Flipper drinks too much and starts laughing, he sounds like that television fish that cackles and surfs backwards on its hind fin.

Before Flipper went into the Army, his name was Theron, but along with those boots and uniforms, he came back to Kingstree with a nose that points east and a new name. He makes us call him Flipper. He says he's earned that much, at least.

We drink sodas under the awning and listen to Flipper and watch poor old William Bundrick ride his bike down the center line. William's this tall skin-and-bones retarded boy who somehow taught himself to ride a bike, but rides only on the dotted line painted down the center of the road, like he needs the line for balance. There have been times we've watched William Bundrick squeeze between a county dump truck and a station wagon going in opposite directions, screaming at the top of his lungs, stomping the pedals like a locomotive, his long legs almost hitting him in the chin with every stroke.

Flipper says, "I don't know what we'll do for a spectator sport if that Bundrick boy ever gets run over." But my mother thinks William's watched by a higher power, and I suppose he must be because he's sent more than his share of cars dodging into the ditch, and he's never so much as skinned his knee.

SO MAYBE THE dream gets better.

Maybe what really happens is William Bundrick comes

batting ass down the highway lines towards this open-air sports car driven by a woman wearing a scarf who sings to the radio, throwing her head back and closing her eyes on the high notes. When she jumps back into the verse and checks the road, there's this wild-eyed boy, all arms and legs, on a bike, right off her left fender. She misses him, but finds the ditch for a hundred feet or so, kisses off a drain culvert, and ends up sideways in the highway, looking back over her shoulder through the dust at poor William Bundrick windmilling down the center stripe. Then, she rolls into the station and kills the engine in front of all of us. She unfolds herself from the inside of that sports car, with clots of mud and weeds stuck in the grill, and flashes one of her thighs at us accidentally, because she's all rattled by William Bundrick and forgets how a lady in a skirt gets out of a sports car.

Being in the Army for three months, Flipper has of course come across a few bare thighs himself, he often tells us, as he sips a beer. Some evenings he talks about Mimi, who danced at a pool hall just off the Army base. The Saturday night before Flipper broke his nose on the obstacle course, he and two of his buddies went to the Ponderosa Social Club without knowing exactly what social meant. They walk in, and Mimi's standing above the center pool table, right under the light, her legs spread, one high heel shoe jammed in each side pocket. "So she wouldn't dig up the felt," Flipper says. He never tells us any more than that. Somebody always asks, "What'd she have on?" and Flipper gets a disgusted stare in his eyes and says, "What you reckon a woman who straddles a pool table would wear?"

The dream woman with the sports car might wave her white thigh at us like a surrender flag and step onto the cement patch over the big underground fuel tanks, tilted forward enough on her high heel shoes so that her legs seem tight, as if she's on the verge of running a race.

I crawl under her car and study the last few inches of her shin, until she drops that scarf and bends down to pick it off her foot. "Find any trouble yet?" she asks me, her head cocked to my level.

Trouble? From where we waste time at the crossroads, trouble might drive a sports car and drop a scarf or flash a thigh. Trouble is what our daddies never tell us about. Trouble is a hole you dig so deep, you eventually need help getting out. In Kingstree, maybe it starts off by burping in Miss Byrd's reading class, which buys you a wrist paddling, and grows into something like watching two little black kids hump on each other that summer behind the tobacco barn.

We were surprised more people didn't see them, or hear them for that matter, squealing "louder and hotter than a couple of stuck dogs in July," Flipper said. We'd finished cropping tobacco for the day and loaded the leaves behind the tractor to take to the barn for the stringers. The stringers were black ladies, mostly big ones, with useless skin that wobbled under their arms when they put a fistful of leaves on the wooden sticks. They were all singers, too, and instead of talking to each other, they'd all hum until the odds of the hymnal caught up, and two or three struck up the same tune at the same time. Soon, the whole barn sounded like choir practice, so maybe the singing drowned out the squealing.

We still heard the hymn coming through the back wall of the barn where the shade was. All we wanted was a cool place to drink down a soda, but we came up on Leon Burroughs, who couldn't have been more than twelve or thirteen, pinning some little girl television wrestler-style in the chickweed. We never saw her again. Both of them naked, sweaty-shiny even in the shadow of the barn, they whimpered like a couple of pups. We crouched, peering around the side of a fertilizer trailer parked behind the barn, our sodas turning hot in our hands. Flipper appeared out of nowhere behind us and snatched who he could grab by the neck and tossed a couple of us back into the sun. We ran the opposite way, and the sodas fizzed out of the bottles as we took off for the woods to talk about Leon Burroughs.

That was trouble. Because by the time we went home for supper, Flipper had already told our parents what we'd been spying on behind the barn, and most of us got whipped for watching. And it wasn't until three or four years later that we found out what all the squealing was about. Still, at the time, we figured Leon ended up with the best end of that deal. The very worst he could get was a whipping too.

IN MY DREAM, I'm a whiz with transmissions. So I put hers back together in an afternoon, and I don't see any trouble with me taking the white sports car out for a spin. "To hear the engine for myself," I tell her. It's near sundown, and she makes me wash my hands before I touch the wheel and kick the oily dirt from my sneakers before I slide into the seat. And she rides too, because she loves that car, and I'm just a stranger who slid underneath it with a wrench. It's Wednesday, and there's some traffic on the highway, heading for mid-week church. *Hymns*, I think to myself, recalling the tobacco barn, double-clutching to make sure the gears work smooth.

We turn around in the edge of a sandy tobacco field so we can head home, and the rear tires spin, then drop deeper into the end of the bare furrow.

"We're stuck," I say, reaching for the door to go check the wheels, like everybody who's ever been bogged down does, as though seeing the hole you're stuck in will bring some revelation. But before I can open the door, she puts a hand on my wrist and says, "It's okay. I think I could sit here all night, it's so nice."

Which makes me think about something Flipper once said. "Don't marry a woman you can't breathe on eye to eye in the morning." He told us this because of the story of him falling in love with a girl he met at the Ponderosa Social Club named Liza. She took him home to her tiny room over somebody's garage, which was fine, he told us, since he knew it was love this time. Love doesn't need fancy things, he told us.

"I couldn't stop staring at her," he said. "She had this movie star mole just above the edge of her mouth and it shifted around when she smiled at me, and," he paused to open a beer, "I got to tell you—she ended up smiling a good bit that evening, if you know what I mean."

The next morning he woke up and snuck a glance at his love Liza in the sunlight and could see that during the night, she'd rubbed her face across the pillow, turning her fake mole into a dark skid mark that ran the width of her cheek. She slept with both eyes strangely half open. "I felt a little betrayed by that mole, I gotta say, but I still checked to see if she was alive, what with those eyes," Flipper said. "Thank god, she was. I wouldn't a known what to do with a body." He left for the base with nothing more valuable than a good piece of advice for down the road.

I wonder what that woman under the scarf would look like after a night in a tobacco field, but I don't wonder long since it's almost dark. The car's so light I can lift and push the back end while she guns the engine, and the tires catch solid ground. We pull back into the station, and the scarf woman goes to the single bathroom behind the sales counter inside. Even though it's near supper time, everyone's waited for us to get back.

"How'd she end up on the driver's side?" Flipper asks.

"What you mean?" I say, and he looks straight at me.

"I mean, you left opposite of how you came back, which means you had to stop somewhere. Why?" And I think how it will sound if I tell them I bogged to the axle in a field, so I just smile, which isn't a lie. Smile and say nothing.

It's a trick I learned from Flipper when he'd stumble into the crossroads on Saturday mornings. "Whatcha do last night, Flip?" He'd just smile and duck his head all the way in the beer cooler. "Where'd you go?"

When he found the coldest one in the ice water at the bottom, he'd answer. "Oh... out and about," and smile again over the top of the can.

For him, out and about usually meant the Golden Leaf Motel, which only has two rooms for actual rent. The rest of the rooms and three of the little cottages out back are for the working girls who show up in the hot months when the tobacco's in. That's the only time of the year that Kingstree does any real business, and those girls who hang around the refrigerator full of beer in the lobby of the Golden Leaf have a nose for business.

So, only two rooms for the occasional person who's lost or has car trouble. We know where the scarf woman will have to spend the night. She says she's too tired to make any more miles in the white sports car and could one of us tell her how to get to the Golden Leaf. But she stares at Flipper when she says this. Like, since he's older, he's in charge of directions. I try hard to see if there's something that flashes between them when he talks, if there're signs we haven't learned yet, but it's too dark to see.

This is where the dream goes bad, and I can't stop it. That night, I sneak to the Golden Leaf. Number Five is empty, so the woman with the sports car must be in number Seven. Through the curtain, I see an outline in the chair I know is Flipper's because of the way he throws out his elbow when he tilts his beer.

It's not the first time I've watched him through the motel window. Once before, we were three deep outside, switching places to get a good shot through the thin slice of space between the shade and the frame. The girl Flipper was with that time reached across toward the little bed table and turned the travel alarm so she could read the hands. Then, she pushed Flipper off of her. We heard him mumble hard. She shook her head, winding up the little alarm clock. Flipper spit on the bed and left, slamming the door to the cottage.

But in my dream, he goes quietly this time, turning back to tip his beer can at her as he leaves. He heads for the other cottages, and I knock on her door. Inside, she winds her own alarm clock and fiddles with her bathrobe and tells me I resemble her own son, which is not exactly what I want to hear because it suddenly makes her tired and out of place in a sports car or a motel room. But she tells me her boy was a mistake she stopped crying about ten years ago.

I ask her why she's on the road—this road anyway—and which way she's going, but she keeps talking about how her son's hair's cut the same way mine is and how he always loved to work under her sports car, too.

While she goes on and on, pausing only to sip from a plastic flask now and then, I see the shadows of familiar heads outside the window that keep bobbing and moving for a good look through the shade, which is fine by me. My friends can look all they want. It won't do my reputation anything but good to be in a sad lady's motel room. She turns off the light and says she needs to sleep. In the dark, she says she's always wanted to pick up a hitchhiker.

Flipper used to pick up hitchhikers regularly along the highway until the afternoon he stopped for this dark-haired boy walking south. Flipper told us he knew the fellow was trouble the minute he sat down in the truck. Said the boy looked to be foaming at the mouth onto his flannel shirt like he had the rabies. They drove for about a hundred yards. Then the boy said, "This is the wrong way," and pulled out one of those little two-shot derringers they use in western movies. Flipper made a U-turn and drove all the way to Raleigh before the hitchhiker fell asleep. Flipper grabbed the gun and the car keys and ran for the police, but they never found the hitchhiker, who left a smell in Flipper's truck that never went away.

I imagine the Golden Leaf Motel has an early check-out time—nine o'clock—so at a quarter of, I'm sitting on top of my brown two-suiter at the crossroads, knowing that to get anywhere important, she'll have to come through this intersection. A trucker stops to give me a ride, but I have to turn him down. In fact, when he asks me where I'm headed, I can't answer him. Poor William Bundrick flies through the center of the crossroads with his eyes shut, listening for cars, I suppose. She eventually downshifts by me, her head wrapped in her scarf, and she seems to be fighting the wheel. I don't think she notices me until she stands on the brakes and cranes her neck for the rear-view mirror.

Walk, I say to myself. Running to her car won't prove anything.

I strap my suitcase on the trunk lid and climb in. The seat's in the same place it was last evening, after the tobacco field. She doesn't say a word as we ride by the station. She waves at the guys behind the pumps on the porch. Flipper tips his beer. I just stare without blinking. I'm going out big. I don't wave because Flipper told me the one thing he learned in the Army, always let folks think you know exactly what you're doing, even if you're dreaming.

WATCHING

IN THOSE DAYS, WE COOKED WHATEVER LEWIS SHOT.
I remember eating sparrows, blue jays. Even a thrush that tasted
tough and rubbery—each bird charred a little on the edges and
hot to the touch. Lewis always built the fire with a handful of
dry leaves or pine straw and a couple of long fireplace matches
he stole off the mantel in his house. While the leaves smoked and
sucked at a flame, Lewis wandered off, twirling his pellet gun,
pumping it until the plastic handle squeaked under the pressure.

He sat with his back propped against the base of a tree,
staring at the highest leaves without moving his head, waiting for something to land in the branches. Sometimes, he just
aimed and fired wildly at a flick of color in the Spanish moss.
Other times, he was more careful and sighted down the barrel
for a minute or so before squeezing off a decent shot in the
direction of movement he thought he saw. But he never took
his eyes from the trees, and that, he said more than once, is
why we always had a bird for the fire. He told us that a bird

does two things straight down: shit and die. The ones he shot usually fell close enough to catch barehanded, like a fly ball, before they hit the ground.

Cal and I were the only ones left building fires and eating birds with Lewis. The rest of the boys on our block were victims of leaf smoke and their mothers' keen noses. I'd been in the woods with Lewis enough to know how to stay upwind and keep the hot part of the fire between me and the funnel of thick, almost-green smoke. That way, my mother could bury her nose in my shirt and smell lots of things, like maybe the school lunchroom or recess or that girl from math class in the process of discovering eau de toilet, but she wouldn't be able to sniff out the fire or the gamey smell of the meat I'd eaten. Cal and I spent most of the time circling the fire, dodging smoke, watching Lewis spin and roast a naked bird on the end of a stick.

Cal was a lot bigger than I was, but he was dumber and slower, and his eyes were set way apart, almost to the sides of his face. He still had the near-white scar on his cheek where the boy from Nicholtown hit him with a rock during baseball season. Every now and then, I had to push Cal to a safe spot, out of the smoke. I'm not even sure he understood why he was moving around and around on his haunches. That was part of the problem. We never thought to worry about things when Lewis was around, especially in the summer when we had no school and plenty of time.

One Friday night, the air was too hot and thick with bugs to shoot basketball behind Lewis' house, and we were bored throwing tennis balls into the sky and watching the bats chase them all the way to the pavement. The Goldens saved us with another one of their parties. The Goldens were the richest people, actually the only rich people on our block. Their son had been gone for years, except on the holidays, and all the money they used to spend on him now floated around untouched, so the Goldens threw lots of big, quiet parties attended by expensive people from out of town, people who appeared in our neighborhood for only the few hours of the party.

The folks on our block watched from porch swings while long cars with thick smoky-colored windows and shiny tires pulled into the Goldens' circular driveway. It was one of the things we did—spying on these parties from some low trees behind the patio. Lewis taught us how. We would keep long, silent vigils, passing potato sticks through the leaves, wondering how it happened, that men and women who were complete strangers knew how to dance with each other. This bothered me.

Thin women who stared into the painted tiles on the patio floor always attracted men who, after only a minute or two of chit chat, led them off through the crowd like a shadow, the both of them sharing a secret code for their hands and feet and head. No one who danced stumbled at the Goldens' parties or stepped on toes. And they held each other like they were related, like they meant to touch. Cal tried to tell us that everyone took the same kind of dance lessons, no matter what town they lived in, but nobody believed Cal, ever.

We hadn't expected a party that Friday, but when the long cars rolled past our houses, Lewis smiled and trotted off. The guests gathered in front of the Goldens' house, just inside the double doors. This made it easy for me and Cal to follow close behind Lewis and sneak through the maze of neighborhood paths to the back of the Goldens' yard, where the woods butted close to the patio wall. We headed for the trees, but Lewis was too jumpy for simple spying. He decided the three of us should see if we could flood a fancy cocktail party.

He found a healthy length of hose behind a shed at the side of the Goldens' lot and told me to screw it into a spigot near the cement fishpond that Mrs. Golden stocked with fat, splotched goldfish and something big from Japan. We duck-walked below a dark line of hedges between the woods and the cement lip of the patio. Beneath that lip, the tiled floor of the patio actually lay below ground level a couple of feet, making the area seem like a huge, shallow bathtub. Lewis snaked the end of the hose through the branches in the bushes and just barely over the lip, then motioned us to go back to the woods. He turned the spigot on very low, so the trickle of water would slowly and quietly fill the patio.

Our spying trees stood at the other edge of the patio, and from there, we watched the water ease like a slow tide across the tiles, picking up stray leaves or a balled up cocktail napkin with its tiny wake. For a long time no one noticed, then the water seeped into someone's shoe, probably into the open toe of a woman's fancy sandal. Cal giggled with his mouth full and passed me a handful of the potato sticks he smuggled in his shorts.

The dancers lost control of their feet, trying to avoid the water, which by now inched deeper and deeper inside the walls of the patio. No one thought to look for a leak in the patio wall or look for the reason their feet were wet. The couples bumped into each other or slid like skaters just learning how to handle ice. One man stood perfectly still beside a table in the center of the patio. He wasn't dancing or lifting his feet out of the puddle. He was twirling ice around and around in a tall glass, and he searched the trees until his stare landed right on us. Cal saw the man too, and his tree limb shook when he tried to shinny farther back in the leaves.

"It's too dark to see us," Lewis hissed at him. "Do what I tell you. Just keep still."

But the man's eyes riveted us, and I knew how a possum felt, frozen in the beam of a flashlight. Cal began to cry, fighting his hold on the limb, and he fell out of the tree. He landed on his hands and knees, and without wasting a motion, crawled through the Goldens' arrangement of perfect shrubs toward the street. In the patio, people scrambled for the higher ground of the Golden house proper, twitching their feet as they ran, like cats with damp paws. The man with the eyes and the twirling drink never moved. He studied me and Lewis in the tree for a few more seconds, then took a couple of soggy steps in the direction of our hiding spot.

I landed hard on my feet and ran low in the shrubs, covering my face. I caught Cal at the edge of his yard. Below his shorts, his knees were black with dirt. He'd rubbed his hands across his shirt and his face, streaking them in a kind of ugly war paint.

"My momma's gonna kill me," he said. Cal worried continuously about his death at the hands of his mother, a stout, loud woman who wanted Cal to be a pianist when he finally grew up.

"You're supposed to get dirty running around playing, especially at night. Tell her you fell down over in my yard," I said. "Why don't you just wash it off?"

"She'll hear the water running and look outside," he said. I wondered what kind of fun you could ever have if you worried about your mother hearing water run and looking over your shoulder, watching you every minute of the day. "Where's Lewis?" he asked in a whisper.

"I guess he stayed in the tree," I told him. "He's too smart to get caught."

We calmed down and walked, hot and sweaty, into Cal's house. His mother smacked her lips and licked her palm. While she groomed the dirt off of Cal with her wet hand, she said, "Son, what have you been up to?"

Cal immediately fell on the ground and grabbed his mother's thick knees. He cried like a boy already whipped as he told her he was so sorry he'd been there when Lewis flooded the Goldens' patio and stopped all the dancers in the middle of their lessons. The part about the lessons confused her, and she cut her eyes to me because she knew I had some sense. I just pointed at my knees, which were spotless, and I didn't get to play with Cal for a while.

All those days, I watched him in his driveway with his baseball cards and pack after pack of firecrackers, blowing up all the pictures of black players. When Cal's momma confined him to the yard, he took it out on black athletes.

The next weekend, before he exploded all the good cards he owned into smelly shreds of paper, his momma let him leave the yard, so we started going back to the woods, eating birds during the afternoon and listening to Lewis tell us what we needed to know about life. Lewis was three years older than we were, already in high school. He played guitar in a band that practiced a couple of times a week inside his daddy's garage. The band knew three songs and knew them well, as far as I can remember. It wasn't much of a song list, but Lewis said that three halfway decent tunes was plenty enough to make girls think you played in a real rock and roll band. He had an older sister named Bunny whose hair and cheeks were bright red, but other than that, the rest of her was the color of white frosting. For almost a year, I'd been watching Bunny undress in her upstairs bedroom window as she prepared for dates. She was a beauty queen at the high school, and it was rare that a weekend passed without Bunny opening the curtains and staring into woods while her arms reached around her at crazy angles, clothes dropping beneath the sill.

Seeing Bunny slide clothes off and on never affected me until the weekend after the deal with Cal and his dirty knees. That Saturday after supper, I laid there on my belly in the azalea bed outside her window, trying to be still, and felt something take over, something different. Spying on Lewis' sister had always been fun, but now it was also uncomfortable. I couldn't move in the pine straw, and I couldn't take my eyes off Bunny, who swayed there, showing off a secret shade of white to me and the world.

I ASKED LEWIS about it the next afternoon because he was older and smarter, but of course I never let on that Bunny was the one in the window. He knew exactly what I was talking about. Between bites of a charred mockingbird, Lewis said, "Hey, you never know when it's gonna hit you—in school, walking down the street, in the morning when you wake up. You gotta be careful in school. About the time you get one, the

teacher looks right at you and says 'Go to the board, Lewis.'
But you're so damn hard you can't blink your eyes. Hard as
Chinese arithmetic. And you walk like a man who's been at
sea for five years. Bad news."

"What you mean by bad?" Cal said. He worried about
bad news. So Lewis told him all the names, nicknames really,
of what to call the thing I felt when Bunny dressed in her
window. Cal started crying, and I couldn't figure out if he was
blubbering because he'd never been on his belly in a flower
bed watching a beauty queen undress herself or because his
mother would kill him if she knew what he was hearing. Lewis
didn't like crying—it made him mad, so he put his cooking
stick down and showed Cal exactly what he meant. He lay
back on the leaves and did all he could to make Cal cry harder.
I thought about Bunny and jerked my head around, watching
for the man with the eyes and the twirling ice who I knew was
looking at us through the trees. There are stories that say you
are never alone in the woods, that someone keeps an eye on
you every second.

Lewis saw me glancing through the trees. "Don't worry,"
he said, then spit in the fire. "I ain't been caught yet. These
woods are 'bout the safest place of all to do it."

He shut his eyes. Cal balled up in the leaves like a puppy,
crying into his shirttail, and Lewis grinned toward the sound,
his eyes closed tight, biting his bottom lip.

Anyway, I learned how to handle the business with Bunny
from the azalea bed when she filled the window with her spotless skin. She didn't have rivet-eyes like the man on the patio,
so I didn't worry about her seeing me or calling my mother
when she finally walked away from the window and headed

downstairs. Most nights, when Bunny undressed for dates, Lewis and his band accompanied her with their three songs, one right after the other. The sound bounced out of the garage and off the thin aluminum siding of Lewis' house and hung a little over the yard, especially when the night air was heavy after a short thunderstorm in the afternoon.

A COUPLE OF days after the lesson in the woods, Cal told his momma about everything Lewis did in front of us at the fire. I'd love to know how it happened. It's not the kind of topic you just bring up at supper or around the TV. Of course, when it came out that Lewis taught us those things, she also discovered we'd been building fires and eating small birds.

Cal's momma, who had always been loud but never violent, kept watch from her kitchen window, and one afternoon she caught Lewis with his back turned in his own front yard. She snatched him by the collar and by his belt and steered him toward the garage door, which was down. At the door, she spun him around and arched up on her tip toes so she could look Lewis right in the eye. I could hear her. She wanted to know who made him the god of the neighborhood who went around telling little boys about what went on inside their pants.

By this time, most of the people living in earshot of Lewis' garage were standing in their doorways, listening to Cal's momma let go on Lewis, who kept turning his head from side to side like Cal's mother was gassing him with her bad breath.

She screamed at him, saying she hoped she was still alive when the sounds of him roasting in hell came sizzling up through the ground. She cocked her knee, jerked it up and dropped Lewis to the driveway. He rolled and made noises like he was going to throw up. While he was down and grabbing for himself, she pulled off a shoe and smacked him a few times on his backside. She said he could tell little boys all about how that felt, little boys who were tricked into making fires and eating birds. Bunny stood in the upstairs window with all her clothes on, twirling the ends of her red hair, watching a mad woman beat up on her little brother.

While his mother screamed, Cal hid across the street, black-player baseball cards and firecrackers in his hands. He took turns laughing and crying because he really did enjoy seeing Lewis bullied, but he also knew that he was a condemned boy the second his mother spanked Lewis in public.

But he never figured Lewis would be so patient. Cal tried to protect himself by staying in the driveway or in the side yard nearest his back door. And for almost a week, he survived without having to run into the house, even when Lewis walked out of his front door, looked across the street and smiled his weird smile. I think Cal relaxed a bit, what with the smiling and the distance between the two of them.

One evening, about the time it became hard to see without lights on, Lewis snuck up behind Cal, who was blowing up some outfielders, and dragged him across the pavement toward the garage door. Cal didn't make a noise. From behind a pine tree in my front yard, I could see the matches still in Cal's hand, and he tried to light one so he could burn Lewis, but everything was moving too fast for a tiny motion like striking a matchbook. Lewis pinned Cal to the garage door and began slamming his head against the aluminum again and again. Cal's eyes rolled once and shut. It looked like his neck just gave up and let his head wobble any way Lewis shoved it.

After a minute of this, Lewis stopped and stroked Cal behind both ears, gently, with a soft touch like a woman's, so that Cal would open his eyes and think the beating was over. The second Cal came back to life, Lewis started again with the back of the head on the aluminum. It was one of the strangest fights I'd ever seen in the neighborhood. No one screamed. Cal seemed to accept the fact that he had to pay for the pleasure of seeing his mother rough up Lewis.

I moved from behind the tree and looked toward Cal's house. A couple of lights were on, but I saw no shadows behind the curtains. It would take a minute or so to find his mother, so instead, I crossed the street and ran to the garage door to try and help Cal. Lewis' back was to me, and over his shoulder, I saw the whites in Cal's eyes flutter. I thought he was about to die. Lewis whirled around.

He dropped one hand from Cal's neck and shook it at me. "You want some of this too?" he hollered, then turned back to Cal and began to bang his head again, a steady, muffled pounding that I might have mistaken for band practice if I hadn't been standing there, watching the two of them. I wondered where all the people were. Bunny's window was dark, and I could barely make out Cal's driveway. I wondered if someone could tell, from a distance, whose side I was on.

Finally, Lewis let him fall to the ground. When nothing happened, when Cal just stayed curled up on the cement, Lewis reached down and pried the matchbook from Cal's fingers. He opened it, lit a single match, then set fire to the whole pack. When he dropped them to the driveway, Cal's face glowed for a second in the burst of yellow flame.

"Go on outta here," he yelled and kicked Cal with a bare foot in the rear end. "You too." And he took a few quick steps toward me. I ran for my yard. When I knew I was safe, I turned and watched Cal stumble across the street, his head down, trusting his feet to find the way home.

That next weekend Lewis and Bunny and their daddy moved out of the house. No one really cared why they left, but most figured it had something to do with Lewis' father, who left for work early each afternoon, even on the weekends, and only came home to sleep through the morning. We all guessed he found a new job with normal hours. But the move couldn't have been a surprise to Lewis. He must've known it was coming. That's why he was so calm while he bided his time with Cal. He knew he could get in the last shot and vanish. Early one morning, four pickup trucks pulled into their driveway, and by dusk the house was empty, except for the cobwebs and dead bugs in the corners of all the rooms. The little dust puppies skittered across the floor when Cal and I opened the front door and snuck in the house that same night. It was the first time we'd seen the inside. All the lights still worked, and it seemed like nobody took much time to clean the place while they lived there.

Cal found a squirt bottle of ketchup in a greasy cabinet and smeared dirty words, the couple he knew how to spell, across the white walls in the living room, big bloody letters that dripped watery streaks the length of the wall. I heard him laughing even when I reached Bunny's room. I saw the four round dents in the carpet where her bed had been set up and another set of marks where a narrow shelf spanned the length of one wall. From the window, I stared below, into the azalea bed, and remembered.

Earlier that week, before they moved, Bunny'd had one last date. It caught me by surprise because it happened on a Wednesday, and she never went out in the middle of the week. Just by luck, I caught a glimpse of her upstairs light when I walked into my yard after supper. I ducked into the woods and snuck through the briars and vines until I was even with her house. I crouched for a minute at the edge of her back yard, then ran for the flower bed at the side of the house, below her window. I watched her stare for a long time at the tops of the trees, like she might have spotted something important, something she should remember. She pulled the red hair over her shoulder, held it up with one hand and brushed the ends. Slowly, she dropped her head and looked down into the azaleas.

She waved at me with both hands, and in the few seconds before I jumped up and ran for home, I wondered if we should all close our eyes, if it had all been too much to see.

MATTHEWMARK
LUKEANDJOHN

THE FIRST MORNING OF VACATION BIBLE SCHOOL, William Bundrick's mother dragged him in late, pulled him through the door by his coat collar like a bad dog. William Bundrick's mother was always bringing him places late, as though running behind was the only pace they possessed. It took William a good ten seconds to realize where he'd ended up. Then he spotted a couple of faces he recognized, smelled the moldy hymnals and rubber cement, saw Miss Angie. Something clicked in his syrup-slow brain, and he recognized where he had landed. To celebrate, he screamed out the names of the four gospels. His mother thumped his ear. She breathed hard, like she had run up the single flight of steps carrying William across her shoulders.

"Paid the registration fee, paid in cash, ahead of time," she announced to the entire room. William Bundrick's mother shifted the air in front of her when she moved. For someone as large as she was, she seemed constantly on the verge of breaking into a sprint, and this made her scary and unpredictable, like a big jungle animal.

Miss Angie was our teacher for the week of VBS. She had no children of her own, although she had not, according to my mother the nurse, passed the age of practical conception. She lived by herself in a small, brown-brick house within walking distance of the church, and she was so thin you'd catch yourself trying to see right through her. She never wore bracelets because the hands attached to her pencil-sized wrists were too small to sustain jewelry. With her bright red hair, my mother said she resembled an unstruck matchstick. Miss Angie's face blushed the color of her hair when William Bundrick's mother advanced on her.

"Paid my fee, so it don't matter if we're late, so here," she said, again to no one in particular. She gave her boy a shove to the center of the room, where he caught his balance and turned a circle, staring down the faces staring back at him.

"Matthewmarklukeandjohn," he repeated. "Matthewmark-lukeandjohn."

"We are all glad you're here, Mrs. Bundrick," Miss Angie said. "And William, too."

"Paid in full," Mrs. Bundrick answered and retreated toward the door, the large tent of a skirt flowing behind her. She shook a finger at William. Her face glistened a little from a coating of sweat. "And you stay put," she said.

William was the most well-known retarded boy in town. There were several others, black and white, but none of them had mothers who took them (late) around town to baseball games and movies and Vacation Bible School. That first day, William wore a suit that stank of moth balls. He'd been scrubbed clean, his skin pink and gleaming and smelling of brutal soap. Unlike his mother, he'd not yet begun to sweat. Tall and gangly, his suit pants were inches too short for his legs. I could see the worn marks on his socks, just above the heels of his shoes, which, from where I sat, looked to be freshly shined.

"Would you like to take your coat off, William?" asked Miss Angie. She didn't want to tell him that shorts and t-shirts were fine this week.

"Nome," William said.

"You'll get hot soon. Not much breeze up here." Miss Angie was trying to be simple and cheerful, recovering from her brush with Mrs. Bundrick.

"Nome."

"Well, have a seat. We were about to begin assigning parts in our little play."

"I do like to play," he said.

"And play you shall, William. Now, have a seat."

Of course, he sat down beside me. And he put his arm around me then leaned in. "Batter up," he whispered. I felt my face go red as his stale breath poured over me, bacon in there somewhere.

WILLIAM BUNDRICK AND I had been on the same baseball team for two straight summers. Kingstree Manufacturing sponsored our team, but our coach wasn't with the company. He was actually the assistant manager at the bank downtown.

When we won, he'd load us up in his blue pick-up and drive us to his bank, unlock the Coke machine with his big ring of private keys, and give us all the bottles of soda we could drink.

That particular summer, I thought William had given up baseball until his mother showed up at practice one afternoon, announced she had bought him a new glove with S&H Green Stamps, and drove away in her Country Squire Wagon before the coach could ask for the registration fee or an insurance form, which he soon discovered were signed and stapled to the front of William's t-shirt.

William was about what you would expect in a ballplayer. When he was in the field, he sang songs that nobody else knew the words for, and he ate blade after blade of new grass. Once, he threw up green on the dugout step. During a game the previous season, as he daydreamed in the outfield, a batter launched a lazy fly ball in his direction. By some fluke of fate and coincidence, William glanced at the sky just in time to raise his glove and keep the ball from beaning him in the forehead. He didn't realize he had actually caught something until we yelled for him to check his glove. After the game, his mother demanded that she be given the baseball he caught as a souvenir.

"I'll pay for it," she said. "Pay in full." She reached into her pocketbook and took out a five-dollar bill, handed it to our coach, then grabbed one of the old, clay-covered practice balls he kept in a plastic bucket. Before she was out of our sight, she handed it to William, who proceeded to wind up and throw it across the parking lot. She dragged him among the cars and trucks, looking for his trophy baseball. "You boys," she screamed at us, "get over here and help William find his special ball."

And we did. We lay down on the gravel, eyeballing beneath the rocker panels. We weren't about to turn the other way when William Bundrick's mother told us to do something. We were afraid of her. For all we knew, William had been normal until she got mad one day and clapped him on the ears too hard. William Bundrick's mother was always mad at something or somebody, maybe the world in general. We just didn't want to get in the way of the anger that boiled out of her. We were smart enough to keep our distance from an angry mother and her retarded son.

WHEN MISS ANGIE talked to us about giving into temptation, that was the day someone taped the sign on William Bundrick's back. The windows of our Sunday school classroom were stretched open wide, trying to allow some moving air to sneak inside. Outside, a group of slow-moving men filled potholes in the church parking lot, so the thick smell of hot tar drifted into the room. Miss Angie used the window as a visual aid. She fanned herself with an old church bulletin and told us to look at the window.

"You see, I'm *tempted* to close that window because the smell of paving tar gives me a horrible headache that will stay with me all evening long, but I know that I must overcome my temptation. Why?" She waited. "Anyone?" she asked.

She conducted during our silence, waving her arms over our heads as she continued to speak. "Why, because it would suddenly get too hot with the windows shut. You see, resisting temptation is always for the greater good. That's why you don't steal when you go to Pitts Drug Store, why you don't smoke cigarettes behind your house, why you don't look at National Geographic pictures from the far corners of the world where clothing is as of yet a complete and utter mystery to the natives."

Miss Angie's face flushed high on her cheeks, giving her match head appearance more depth than ever. Most of us had already committed one or more of the sins she used as examples, often simultaneously. But we weren't bad kids. We were just young and weak and curious and normal. We were simply strangers to temptation. At least I think that's what Miss Angie would have said about us.

She talked about Jesus and his resistance to all flavors of temptation. Outside, the men had their shirts off, sweating over the steaming tar. I could taste asphalt on the roof of my mouth. "My, the time!" Miss Angie said. "Clean up quickly. Your mothers will be here in a minute."

Angel shapes and the cut-out remains of some activity loosely related to temptation littered the floor. We scooped all of this up, put the rubber cement and scissors and staplers in the correct cubbyholes, waited for Miss Angie to release us to the heat outside. William walked by, and I saw it there, across the broadest part of his shoulders, like an athlete's name: a neatly lettered index card that read, *Crazy Freddie*.

We all saw. William passed close enough for me to touch it. Miss Angie didn't see a thing, of course. That would require a different alignment of the planets, a different kind of fate. Instead, William Bundrick walked out of the church and into the sunshine with his new name tag, walked right past the men tamping tar flat with giant, metal spatulas, slid into the hot back seat of his momma's Country Squire, and had no clue that temptation had reached up and scotch taped itself across his shoulders.

William didn't show at baseball practice that afternoon. Our coach asked if he were sick or on vacation. William never missed practice or the Saturday games. Our banker coach didn't know that William was always sick, always sniffling up a runny nose or coughing like a car engine. So, yes, he was sick, but that wasn't anything new. And no, the Bundricks never went on vacations. Mr. Bundrick was a mystery that had long since disappeared, and William's mother only had enough energy and money to take her son places and drop him off.

We practiced without him, keeping our eye on the parking lot, waiting for the Country Squire to roll into sight. I knew they wouldn't show. I can't tell you *how* I knew it. I just did. Like the way you know it's going to rain before you see drops hit dirt.

I COULDN'T RAISE up my eyes the next morning when she came through the door again, pulling William by the ear. I felt the rush of her as she led him into the middle of the room, toward Miss Angie's desk. "Just what in the world are you teaching them?" she yelled, waving in our direction. "Where are you getting these kinds of lessons?" William smiled at her. "Are you evil?" she said.

The blood left Miss Angie's face. There were too many questions to answer. She could only ask questions in return. "Them in reference to whom?" she whispered. "What?"

"Them whoms." William Bundrick's mother turned on us. Her glare was watery-eyed, as though she were in the midst of an allergic attack. She pointed a finger at us, the back of her arm swinging heavy and hammock-like. "I know all about this," she said, and held up the *Crazy Freddie* sign. "You think I don't know? I know all about you."

William Bundrick nodded his head non-stop, agreeing with everything and nothing in particular. We had nowhere to run, and each of us except one, had no *reason* to run. Mrs. Bundrick created a sudden gauntlet of accusation, walking around the room, pointing at each face. "You? Was it you?" she asked one of the girls in the class, at the far end of the room. Immediately, the girl said, "No, ma'am." William Bundrick's mother asked the next person if he had put the sign on her son. Again, the answer was no.

Miss Angie caught up with her breath and sucked up enough air to speak. "Mrs. Bundrick, this isn't necessary, nor is it fair treatment for the children."

"You don't want to talk to me about fair. Sit down and be quiet." Miss Angie melted slightly into her chair, looking even smaller than normal. William Bundrick's mother continued her interrogation, working her way toward me. When she was only a couple of questions from my place on the floor, I decided I would say something else, offer up an answer instead of a simple no. I would show her what I had learned. This was the last day of Vacation Bible School. Miss Angie had taught us things. I could put one of them to practice here. Mrs. Bundrick moved down the gauntlet. She finally reached me. She brought her head close to mine. I could tell she recognized me from baseball. "I don't have to ask you," she said just loud enough for the class to hear. "You're on William's team." She turned to the next boy.

"Yes, you do," I said too loudly. She stopped and turned slowly. "You should ask me."

"What did you say?" Her eyes rolled slightly.

"Mrs. Bundrick, you need to leave." Miss Angie was gaining strength, if not conviction. "We can settle this another way."

"What did you say?" Mrs. Bundrick acted as though she hadn't heard Miss Angie.

"I said, you need to ask me about it."

She struggled to keep the anger corralled in her face. I thought she might cry. "Why would I want to ask you?"

"Because," I answered her. I had to pause to decide on the next words to say. "Because I have something to tell you."

She searched my face. The entire room went quiet. The air didn't move. She cocked her head slightly, like a dog puzzling over a new, high-pitched noise. Before I could explain that I knew absolutely nothing about the sign, before I could tell her what I *did* know about temptations and trouble they could cause for the greater good, before I could tell her I'd had a chance to peel that sign off her boy's shoulders and didn't take it, she drew her hand back and hit me flush on the jaw.

I saw it coming. But it took seconds and seconds, it seemed, for her hand to carve that gentle arc from her shoulder to my cheek. She hit me with the flat, fleshy part of her hand, something between a slap and a right hook. A light flashed in my eyes, and the force in that heavy arm knocked me off my chair. Someone screamed. Miss Angie jumped from her desk and ran toward William Bundrick's mother, who already had William by the ear, tugging him into the hallway. She had found out what she thought she needed to know.

"What are you doing?!" Miss Angie yelled.

"Matthewmarklukeandjohn," William yelled back, the names of the gospels fading in the hallway.

I stared up at the faces above me. The piece of hard candy in my mouth floated toward my throat and I started to gag, then I remembered I wasn't eating candy. I spit a tooth into my hand, a molar still bloody at the root, and I tongued the empty hole in my gum where the tooth used to be.

After I washed my mouth out in the bathroom, Miss Angie caught me in the hallway. Her face color was back to normal. "I'm so sorry," she said, "about your tooth. I'm so sorry this happened."

"It's okay, Miss Angie," I said.

"I have to ask you this. Why did you do it?"

"Lose my tooth? Well, she hit me."

"No, why did you put the sign on William? It wasn't very Christian." Miss Angie tried to give me a glare, but it came off looking like she had a pain in her side.

"I didn't do it, Miss Angie," I said. "Swear."

"But you all but confessed to Mrs. Bundrick."

"I was just trying to tell her I was sorry for not pulling the sign off his back when he walked out the door that day. I didn't stick it on there. I wanted to tell her about temptation."

"She struck you for no reason?" Miss Angie drew in her breath quickly. Her voice went high and squeaky.

"She probably has some reasons. We just don't know about all of them, I guess." I remember that moment as being the first time I ever said anything that confused an adult. Up to that point, most of the things I said were either amusing or boring to grownups. They either laughed or pretended to be interested or simply ignored me. But that second, when I said something slightly mysterious, I stunned Miss Angie. She couldn't answer. Amid the lessons on temptation and sin and faith, this was the most important thing I learned the week of Vacation Bible School: that it was entirely possible to confuse someone into complete silence.

THE NEXT MORNING, my tooth was all but forgotten. I showed it to my parents, but didn't tell them how I happened to be missing a molar. They slid a dollar under my pillow that night, but couldn't find the tooth, because I had hidden it in my baseball glove.

The field smelled like baseball season that day, wild onions mixed with the wet funk of boiling hotdogs. Once morning moved along, the creosote in the railroad ties began to heat up along the tracks and the bitter odor floated over the field like a fog. I had re-oiled my glove the week before and the scent of saddle soap hit my nose every time I waved at the fly that buzzed my ear. The second inning was when it all broke loose. That's when William and his mother pulled up and ran toward the dugout, her screaming about how he'd paid his fees, so it didn't matter if he was late or not. She shoved him onto the bench and took her usual spot in the bleachers, just behind home plate.

William waited for us to come in from the field, sitting on the bench, eating the last couple of bites of a Baby Ruth. "Batter up," he said when we filed in. Our coach liked to get William's at-bat out of the way early while the game was still yet to be decided. "Grab a stick, Bundrick. Get your cuts, son," he said in his most non-banker voice.

Just as William shoved his head inside a plastic helmet and found his favorite bat, the sheriff's department car pulled up behind the stands. Miss Angie rode in the front seat with the new deputy, Wesley, who spent most of his days making sure kids didn't get run down at the elementary school crossing. He wanted to be anywhere but here. Miss Angie was different. She appeared almost fearless and somehow suddenly heavier, like she had gained gravity. She jumped out of the car and walked quickly toward the stands, then stood, pointing at William Bundrick's mother.

We couldn't really hear from the dugout, but my mother told me after the game that Miss Angie simply said to the deputy, "That's her. You know whom I mean. She hits children. In a church, no less." The air stopped moving again.

The deputy was uncomfortable around so many grown-ups. "Missus Bundrick, why don't you come with me for a second," he said very quietly, trying to be as unnoticeable as possible.

"My boy's playing ball," she said without taking her eyes off the field.

"You see how she acts," Miss Angie said. "Brazen disregard. Utterly brazen."

"Missus Bundrick, you need to come on with me, hear?" Wesley raised his tone. He flexed his weight lifter arms some, stretching the hem on his uniform sleeves.

"My boy is coming up to bat. I need to see him swing," she answered.

Then, according to most accounts, Miss Angie shoved Wesley forward with both her spindly arms, and he kept moving toward William Bundrick's mother. He reached for her arm, and Mrs. Bundrick slapped him quickly on the wrist. "That's what made him use the handcuffs," my mother said

later. "That was the act of somebody who wanted some attention." My mother believed much of the known world revolved
around how much attention you either got or didn't get. For
her, all actions or reactions were a result of this overabun-
dance or inadequacy. No one, I discovered, ever received the
perfect amount of attention. That was impossible.

"You see how she hits," Miss Angie called out. "For no
reason."

"William Bundrick!" his mother yelled as the deputy tugged
on her elbow. "You go, William Bundrick."

William stood in the on-deck circle near the dugout, taking
vicious practice swings at imaginary pitches. He heard his
mother, then stuck his finger in the earhole of his batter's
helmet, trying to dig out the voice.

Mrs. Bundrick squirmed to break Wesley's grip. He had the
handcuffs on one of her floppy arms. He couldn't catch the
other one as it wind milled by, so he just dragged her. The
people in the rickety stands shifted to safer positions, closer
to each other, like a covey of scared quail. The deputy and
Mrs. Bundrick made their way out of the wooden bleachers
and toward the patrol car. She never quit screaming. "William
Bundrick, you see what they're doing to your momma? You
remember this, boy."

William waved at her. The fact that his mother was being
hauled away by a large deputy sheriff, whose face was turning as red as Miss Angie's hair, seemed to please him. He
smiled broadly and waved again. "Hey, momma," he called
out. "Matthewmarklukeandjohn!" From inside the dugout,
our pitcher asked William through the fence if his mother had
killed somebody.

"Nossir," he said. Our coach told everybody to shut up.

Miss Angie called out to anyone who would listen that she would watch William until "the whole situation" was all sorted out. "He's in good hands. I'm not heartless, you know. I just want some justice for our young people. I had to take a stand." The parents sitting there were confused enough to stare, but not worried enough to ask questions. They would try and fill in the blanks later. They probably didn't want to ruin a nice Saturday morning.

The umpire yelled play ball, and we were at it again. I was beginning to get used to wild, important things happening, then feeling them drift quickly into memory or legend. I get slapped and lose a tooth and ten minutes later, we're building a clay model of the parting of the Red Sea. William's mother gets hauled off to jail, and before the patrol car is out of sight, we're taking our swings at the plate. No harm, no foul. Same with William. He wasn't smart enough to be fazed. "Batter up," he told himself, and walked to home plate, his pants already dirty with red clay, though he'd only been in the ball-park a few minutes.

"You ready, son?" the umpire asked him.

"Batter up," William repeated.

When William Bundrick stepped into the batter's box, we knew what to expect. We knew he'd grab a handful of red dirt with one hand, spit into the other several times, then create a kind of gritty paste that he'd wipe on the thighs of his baseball pants. He'd take several ferocious practice swings, gyrations so wild, the umpire would pull the catcher out of the way. Once he settled in, William would eye the pitcher and swivel his hips slightly. Always, William was in the batter's box for only three pitches. Each time the pitcher wound up, William would clamp his eyes shut and chop at the air in front of the plate. And each time, the ball ended up in the catcher's mitt. Except this time. Because this time, he did something we had never witnessed. William Bundrick made contact. The ball stung off the very end of his bat, squibbing a few inches foul outside the third base line. William stood there in the batter's box, shaking his hands, surprised not that he'd hit the ball but that he had some sort of painful, electric buzz running through his hands. Once the pain subsided, just seconds later, he searched for the ball. The crowd, their attention pulled back to the game from the recent noisy incarceration, watched in near silence as William danced inside the batter's box. He was more addled than usual.

Miss Angie was the first to say it. From where she had anchored herself behind home plate, she yelled at William Bundrick, "Run!" Then repeated it: "RUN!" William turned, looking for the voice, the one that didn't sound anything like his mother, then searched for the ball, which had come to rest against the chain link fence just beyond our dugout. "Run!" she screamed, this time joined by some other parents. We took up the chant in the dugout, even though we knew it was a foul ball.

William Bundrick's brain made a connection with his legs, and he dashed the wrong way down the third base line, all of his limbs churning cartoon circles, his tongue wagging. He hit third and turned for second, where he slid in a blast of red dust, scrambled to his feet and searched for first. He rounded first widely, then dug for home and dove across the plate. When he rose to his feet, he pronounced himself safe and grinned at the crowd. Miss Angie's voice cut through the rest. "Excellent, William," she said. William raised his arms the way he'd seen ballplayers celebrate on television. The umpire shrugged and called him safe as well. Like I said, William was the best-known retarded boy in town, well-known enough to get away with a foul ball home run.

Miss Angie walked to our dugout, where William was breathing hard and digging through the dirty practice base-balls, trying to find one to take to his mother, another souvenir. "She'll pay for it. So it's alright. She got money."

"William?" Miss Angie said through the fence.

"Yessum?" he answered.

"Come with me. I'm going to take you to my house and you can wait for your mother there. They'll bring her when she's through."

"I hit it, Miss Angie. I hit that ball."

"I know, William. I was watching. Now, come with me. We can't be late." The two of them headed across the parking lot. We saw William throw his baseball over the tops of the cars. We decided they could look for that one by themselves.

The sheriff gave William Bundrick's mother a fine, a small one, for knocking out my tooth and told her that she would have to go see the Methodist minister for six Thursday afternoons in a row to learn about controlling her anger. She paid her money in full for the anger management lessons, but never did go see Reverend Scoggins. If my parents actually found out she was the one who knocked out my molar, they never let on. It wouldn't have been worth the energy anyway. And nobody confessed to putting the sign on William Bundrick's back. I could guess who did it, at least narrow it down to two or three people. The letters were so neat and perfect. It was somebody who cared about penmanship. But finding out wouldn't have made any difference either. That's the way we lived in that place those days. Things—sometimes bad, sometimes good—happened, but the weight of time beat them all down, like those men tamping tar in potholes. All of our rights and our wrongs got patched up and smoothed away, sooner or later.

The only person who didn't get rolled over was Miss Angie. She moved not long after Vacation Bible School, before the end of summer. The last we heard, she had put on some weight, and there was a rumor she had found someone to marry her. For some reason or the other, everyone lost touch with her all together.

BODIES THAT DRIFT IN THE RIVER FLOW

SOMETIMES YOU KNOW THINGS BEFORE YOU KNOW THINGS. Mrs. Tisdale comes to the door, and I know something is wrong. I know. From the top bunk of my bed, I watch her coming up the sidewalk, walking fast but walking like a woman who is already lost, her skirt moving quickly around her, like a wave to anyone who spies through the window.

I know the doorbell won't ring. She is not a bell person. She is too good a friend of my mother's to announce herself that way. She knocks once and opens the door. What she doesn't know is the bell doesn't work anyway. It is shorted out somewhere along its line and my father has never pulled the wires and traced down them to find the problem. I hear Mrs. Tisdale's voice flow up the staircase, so faint I can barely make it out, strained and pitched higher than normal. Her voice sounds like an animal she is trying to keep on a leash, trying to make it heel. Because her voice wants to run away from her. I hear my mother fall back on her nurse's voice, that healing tone. I climb off the top bunk and move closer to the doorway.

"Now, Roberta, we shouldn't jump to conclusions," my mother says. "Let's not worry until we have something to worry about."

"Something's gone wrong," Mrs. Tisdale says. "I feel it."

I know what she means. Lonnie was supposed to meet me in the back corner of the field behind the school. I'd told him I'd stolen a package of Apple Jack chewing tobacco that we could try. He didn't even seem excited. He didn't even ask where I got it from. I held it in front of his nose and he knocked my hand away, then said he was sorry. "I'll see you there, I guess," he said. He sounded like he was walking through deep mud. Something was pulling at him, something had changed and nobody told me about it. I yelled at him to be there around four o'clock and he waved at me without turning around. Now, in my house, I think Mrs. Tisdale and I must have the same dull ache in our stomachs, the same idea spinning wildly in our heads, that something has gone bad-wrong with Lonnie.

"Can we ask your son about it?" I hear Mrs. Tisdale say, and my mother doesn't see anything wrong with that, but she doesn't understand what's going on, doesn't catch the dark messages in the air.

She calls me downstairs and when I walk into the little room just off the front door, she says, "Do you feel okay?" She puts her hand on my forehead. "You're pale. And clammy." Mrs. Tisdale looks me in the eyes, and I think she might find something lurking there.

"Have you seen Lonnie?" she says, still locked on my eyes. I glance at my mother and she nods at me.

"I saw him just before school was over," I say. I have a hand in my pocket, fingering the block of chewing tobacco. "We were going to meet at four. At the soccer goal."

She's still staring at me until my mother breaks up the silence. "So he didn't show," she says, and it doesn't sound like a question.

"No, ma'am," I say and Mrs. Tisdale's eyes begin to cloud over and fill with water. I think that the Apple Jack will change something—the mood, the sound the voices are making in the echoey little room. I pull the block out of my pocket. "We were going to try some of this," I say, and Mrs. Tisdale blinks and the tears fall on the front of her dress, and she runs out of the house. My mother doesn't take the chewing tobacco away from me. Tobacco isn't important now.

"She knows it's bad. How's she know that?" she asks me, and I want to tell her that I'm way too young to have answers like that, but not too young to have the same question. "Are you sure you feel okay?" she asks me, palming my forehead again.

"Yes, ma'am," I lie, but it's one of those lies that can't hurt anybody. "Oh, and give me that tobacco," she says. "That stuff is nasty."

Back in my room, I watch the bats come out in the last bit of evening, fluttering above the tree line and chasing bugs all the way to the ground. The last thing that happens, before it goes completely dark: Lonnie's brothers walk through the neighborhood, calling out his name, as if he has maybe fallen asleep somewhere and just woken up, not knowing where he is.

THE NEXT MORNING, my father makes me ride with him to the river to watch the sheriff's deputies drag the river downstream from the bridge. He doesn't say much to me on the ride, but I know I have no choice. This is how he teaches me things. He points me in the direction of the worst of the world and then says, *Avoid shit like that and you'll be alright*.

He does most of his talking to my mother. Arguing. She can't understand why he would want his son to watch men sling giant hooks into the deepest cuts in the river and see what they haul up from the water. "He's only twelve," she says.

"That's exactly why I'm taking him," he says back to her. My mother and I don't understand him, but that is nothing new for us.

On the way to the river, he already has a beer in his hand. "You know Lonnie's gone for good, right? You see what he's putting everybody through, right?" He grips the steering wheel like it might escape, breathing hard through his nose. But he isn't mad at me. I know that now. "What the hell was going through his head? Nothing, that's what. He didn't learn a damn thing the first time." He turns angry when he talks about death. I've never talked about it before, never even heard anyone else talk about it. Death might as well be something like a far-off universe or volcanoes. It just never comes up in conversation, except when my father starts to slur words and tell his Vietnam stories.

By that morning, we'd all heard Lonnie had climbed up on the rail of the metal bridge in broad daylight, in the middle of the afternoon, dressed like he was going to the store or to a party, in jeans and a long-sleeved shirt which didn't make much sense in early June. Nobody wore clothes like that in June, to the river. Then again, none of it made sense. There is a furniture store above the river and a big window that looks out over the water toward the bridge. A salesman saw Lonnie jump and then didn't think a thing of it. Lots of boys jump off that bridge. Even in clothes like that.

"But not in June, not when we haven't had rain in a month," my father says. "God knows what's under the surface."

He parks our Bel Air in the furniture store parking lot. The lot rises a good twenty feet above the river. Below us, sheriff's deputies have anchored their jon boats in several places just off the bank. I watch them brace themselves then whirl the hooks at their side before they launch them into the current. They reel back in what the river will give them. One deputy brings up a tire. Another, what looks like a bedside table. No bodies. Lonnie's father squats on the river bank like a man with nowhere to go.

"I couldn't do that," my father says, pointing at Mr. Tisdale. "I couldn't sit around waiting on the worst. They've already put his wife in bed." He talks quietly, like someone is eavesdropping, but we are the only ones in the parking lot. "She went all hysterical. Gave her drugs."

He thinks I'm listening, and he thinks I'm looking at the river, but I'm staring beyond the banks, down the highway that leads to the country club. Lonnie and I used to fish in a swamp pothole just beyond the only curve in the highway. I try to count the number of times we crossed this bridge on our bicycles.

The water in this river is the color of old coffee, of Coca-Cola, which makes everyone think it is dirty, but this is clean water. I did a report in school. The color of the water comes from trees leaking tannin into the water, cypress trees that line the banks, their knees poking out like soldiers. The water is so dark that you can't see more than a foot or so into it. This river keeps secrets from the people on the bank. Lonnie's father peers into the water like he's going to be able to suddenly see exactly what happened, like the water will clear and be as transparent as the Moose Lodge Pool. I can tell that he is a man who doesn't know exactly what to hope for right now.

Lonnie should have known better than to jump in June. In June the heat begins to raise the river banks and bring all that's bad closer to the surface. It's not a high bridge, but it's high enough. He should've learned the first time he jumped, when he banged his face on that refrigerator and had to have all those operations. Lonnie ended up with a fake eyeball and a rebuilt eye socket. For a while, he was all anybody talked about. Then he just turned into a kid in town with a fake eye and plastic on half his face and nobody ever asked him about it anymore.

One of the deputies balancing in a jon boat lets out a yell and begins tugging quickly on his rope. Something is pulling in the other direction, something more than the current. "Wesley ought not to be that excited," my father whispers and puts his arm around me. Wesley has arms like a weightlifter, and they bulge under his uniform as he fights the river. Mr. Tisdale stands and walks a couple of steps in the direction of the deputy's boat. The deputy acts like a man deep-sea fishing, reeling in slack anytime the shark takes a break. There is a marker on the rope, a bright piece of cloth, tied ten feet from the hook, a warning. I see it appear. Mr. Tisdale cannot decide what to do. He retreats from the water's edge, then turns completely around, toward the parking lot. He sees us watching and begins to wave but thinks better of it. He turns again to the water.

Something tangled in the hooks breaks the river's surface and Mr. Tisdale falls to his knees in the sand, but it's just a big piece of truck tire, something sheared off an eighteen-wheeler. Wesley looks disappointed that he did all that work and only has a hunk of rubber to show for it. He wanted a body—a boy—for his efforts. The deputy is soaking wet from sweat, almost as if he'd taken a dip.

"I've had enough of this," my father says and steers me back toward the car. He tosses his empty can in the bushes. When we climb inside, he says, "You understand this? I want you to understand all this. There are people in boats. There's a daddy on his knees in the sand. There's a couple of people up in a parking lot watching like it's a football game. This isn't supposed to be the way the world works. Not the things children are supposed to cause. You need to understand that." He fires the engine up, and I nod at him but I don't understand any of it. There are too many pieces. It's like the way a huge puzzle looks when you first dump it out of the box, when the pieces are piled on a table, before somebody smart begins to make sense of it. All I know is that Lonnie didn't meet me in the field behind the school and, not long after that, I knew things before I knew them.

IT WAS MRS. Tisdale's idea for all of us to wear our baseball uniforms to the funeral. I didn't know what a pallbearer was. "You're like a special group of friends who might be sadder than anyone else, except for the family. You're like the next rung down from family," my mother says, smoothing away some wrinkles on my jersey with her hands.

"Most of the time pallbearers carry the casket," my father says when she finishes. "I guess they don't think y'all are strong enough." She doesn't even roll her eyes at him like she usually does when he butts in. "Uniforms are a bad idea. Makes this look like a circus," he says.

"She can have whatever she wants because of what she's lost," my mother says and the way it comes out of her mouth, we know it is the last word.

She washed my uniform last night and it smells like Tide. She could wash it a hundred times and the clay stains on the knees would never completely come out, but it smells new, like I have a game that day. "We're not supposed to bring gloves and stuff, are we?" I ask. "Are we supposed to wear cleats?" I wonder if Lonnie is wearing his uniform right now. Number 8.

She shakes her head. "But wear the hat. And wear sneakers." We play for Kingstree Manufacturing. Mr. Sellars, the assistant manager of the bank in town, is our coach. When we win games, he piles us into his pickup and drives us to the bank and lets us have free sodas out of the machine in the back lobby. We can have two if we want. The Coke is the color of the river, and I catch myself thinking of Coca-Cola and river water and baseball and wonder if this is how you begin to put the pieces together, start seeing the connections between things that happened and are happening and might happen the minute you step out in the sun in your baseball uniform and turn left for the church, instead of right for the Youth Center and the baseball field.

The last thing my mother does before we drive to the church is put a clean, pressed handkerchief in the back pocket of my uniform. "You'll need this," she says, and I wonder where it came from. I've never seen anybody in my family use a handkerchief.

On the way to the church, my parents try to talk under their breath, thinking that the open windows and the sound of the engine will be enough to camouflage their conversation. My brother isn't interested. Eli looks out the window and tugs at his bow-tie. He can't understand why he isn't allowed to wear a uniform. He's never been to a funeral either. Beneath the rush of air, I hear my parents talking about what I already know: that Lonnie didn't just jump off the bridge because he wanted to swim. He jumped because he didn't want to come out of the water. In the days since one of the deputies snagged Lonnie and pulled him out of the water, I've eavesdropped on several conversations floating up from my living room, parents worried about what this would do to all of us. Would we be tempted to jump off the bridge? Parents wanting to know why Lonnie was so unhappy. Parents saying the children didn't have enough to worry about to warrant leaping through the air.

I knew I could never jump off that bridge. I'd been there one night, right after Lonnie's first jump, when he banged his head and his eye on something, and I remember looking down into the black that didn't seem to end. I couldn't tell the night from the water's dark surface, and I knew then that I didn't have it in me to jump. I wondered why Lonnie did it in broad daylight.

"Will we have to look at a dead person?" my little brother says, loud enough for everyone to hear.

"No," my father says over his shoulder. "Not after the river." I know what he means. Three days underwater, I'm guessing Lonnie doesn't look like himself anymore.

A WOMAN WHO flutters around like a nervous little animal lines us up just inside the front door of the church, smallest to tallest, like that is important. She tells the first boy in line, our catcher Wendall, that when she taps him on the shoulder, he should walk in slow and a man near the altar will show us which pew to sit in. I didn't know funerals had parades, where we had to walk and look out at a crowd watching us. After we sit, it isn't two minutes before Lonnie's family walks in. His brothers stare at the tops of their shoes when they move. Mr. Tisdale holds up his wife. She sags against him like she is on her last legs. With each step she takes, she lets out a little moan. Mr. Tisdale smiles, but I can tell it isn't real. His eyes give him away.

It has never bothered me to see other people sad, and even this day in the church, Mrs. Tisdale's moans and the way Lonnie's brothers look like they haven't slept in days doesn't make me want to reach for my handkerchief. Even the sight of the coffin, which is built short, the size of most of us in uniform, doesn't get to me. I find myself thinking about baseball and when we'll wear this uniform again and if my mother will wash the funeral out of it before the next game.

No, it's when Reverend Scoggins walks into the pulpit. That's when I begin to know. He doesn't do what he normally does when he starts a sermon. He doesn't pluck his own handkerchief from his robe and wipe his mouth and ask God to make the words of his mouth and the meditations of his heart acceptable in His sight. Reverend Scoggins looks like a man who just wandered onto the saddest chapter in a book.

He begins to talk two or three times, the only thing arriving from his mouth a deep half-croak. He finally pulls his handkerchief from a fold of his robe and wipes his eyes. That's when I feel my own eyes begin to fill. I wonder if Lonnie's fake eye could shed tears. I never asked him that. Where would his tears come from? Would they even be real? I wonder why I am thinking of that now. Reverend Scoggins' shoulders slump forward and he begins to shake under the weight of his sobs. *He is supposed to lead us through this*, I think. I turn slightly and see that the church is full. People near the back stand against the wall, beneath the stained glass. I didn't eat much breakfast this morning. I wasn't hungry enough. But now, I feel a sour taste from my stomach rising in the back of my throat.

If he can't lead us through this, who will? I catch sight of my mother, dabbing at her eyes. My father stares up at the windows, trying to distract himself. He will act mad, I know. He always acts mad when he doesn't know what to do. Reverend Scoggins tries one more time to begin to talk and the words lodge in his throat. At the back of mine, the sour taste rises higher, faster, and I need to let it go somewhere. We are sitting only two pews from the front, so I climb over our left fielder and one of our pitchers and bolt for the door to the side of the altar, run fast like I'm trying to beat out a grounder to short. I pass Reverend Scoggins, and he notices me for the first time and begins to say something. He looks to be mad. I make it to a door, and just inside it, I throw up on the shiny, polished tiles, my eyes watering from the crying and the retching. I smell something sharp, the stuff they use to clean the floors, maybe. Nothing splashes on my uniform, but my hat falls right in the mess, lands right on the KM logo. On the other side of the door, back at the altar, Reverend Scoggins has discovered his voice. "Sometimes God isn't fair," he says. "Just not fair." And I wonder if they'll let me get a new hat.

A hand hard on my shoulder, and I look up expecting to see Mr. Rogan who cleans the church or the secretary at the desk in the preacher's office or someone who will get on me about messing up the shiny, squeaky floor, but I'm wrong. My father is there, and it's not that he has a different look in his eye. It's that he's looking right at me now. He usually stares over the top of my head or back over his shoulder like somebody in black pajamas and a straw hat is going to sneak up on him. Now, he is locked on my eyes like he's trying to read my thoughts.

"I don't think anybody noticed," he says, then sees the floor. "I'd rather you puke than cry your eyes out. At least this is something." He reaches in the back pocket of my uniform, pulls out the white handkerchief and hands it to me. "Wipe your mouth. Let's get out of here. Forget the hat."

I am not sure if pallbearers are allowed to leave before a service is over, not sure of the rules since I've never been one. I know that after the service, Lonnie is being laid in the ground at the big cemetery out on the Sumter Highway, and my parents have been debating all morning whether or not I should go, whether or not it is too much for boys in baseball uniforms to sit through a funeral *and* a burial.

"I don't know," I say and swipe my mouth clean. On the other side of the door, music has started, organ music, and I hear a church full of people trying to sing when they don't really feel like it.

"Don't worry. This is one of those days when you can get away with whatever you want. It's like a strange holiday. Come on," he says. "Your momma will get a ride. No problem."

Outside, the morning sunlight is blinding and moving toward noon. He lets me sit in the front seat, and we ease out of the church parking lot and turn left and ride the easy bluff down the floodplain toward the river. Just when he is supposed to bear right to Scout Cabin and the beach where everybody goes, he steers straight and continues out of town. He sees me swiveling my head, trying to figure out where we are headed. "Relax," he says. "It's something new."

After a mile, he turns down a potholed, two-lane road with wild grass growing right to the edge of the asphalt. I feel us drop downhill a little and the sounds outside the window change. The cicadas pipe up in the heat. I hear them screeching over the hum of the tires on the pavement. Another mile and he turns down a sand road barely wide enough for the car. I wonder what will happen if we meet someone coming the other way, but my father doesn't seem to mind. He takes the curves too fast, and I slide against the door. He makes one more turn, this time into the trees onto what doesn't even look like a road, more like a path that weaves between pines and hardwoods that have never been thinned. Weeds grow high in the path until it suddenly breaks into a clearing and, in front of me, I see a sliver of white beach and the black water of the river as it slows on a bend to the right.

The beach is just wide enough for a rickety picnic table and a small wooden bench that could be used for cleaning fish, I guess. Off the beach, just at the tree line, is a cement platform about the size of a closet. A tarp has been slung over the cement by a network of ropes from several trees. "Nobody really knows about this place," my father says. He doesn't like surprises when they happen to him. He told me once that he'd gotten his share of surprises in Vietnam. "You crawl down a tunnel with a flashlight and a pistol and a fruit bat comes at you in the dark and you crap your pants, that's enough surprise for the rest of your life." But he likes surprising other people, likes making them open their eyes and wonder, *Where the hell did that come from?* He knows he's surprised me.

We sit in the car. "You know all those times I take off and you and your mother think I'm off doing things I shouldn't? Well, I never really go very far," he says. "This is where I come. So now you know."

Outside, the air under the trees is thick and cool and has the dank smell of a swamp. My father doesn't even bother to step behind a tree when he pees, just lets it go right there in the path. "Don't worry. Nobody upstream or down for a mile."

We walk to the sand, and I take off my shoes and my red baseball socks that are stretched up to my knees. "I found this place right after I got out of the service. I knew I'd need something I could keep to myself," he says. The sand is beginning to get hot. To my left, a line of turtles suns on a cypress log that juts out of the shallow water. His shoes are off too. I'd never noticed my father's feet, the way one of his big toes angles in at the joint, like it was broken somehow years ago. Here, the river doesn't make any sound. There's current, but nothing hurried you can see or hear in the black water.

"I want to tell you something," he says. "You can't blame the river for what happened. What happened was going to happen, one way or the other. There's nothing to blame."

A tiny, fast movie runs through my head: me talking to Lonnie, asking him to meet me after school, the dark block of Apple Jack tobacco, the empty school yard with me sitting there long after four o'clock, picking at a hole in the soccer net and there's not enough string left to patch it up. Then the movie changes, and I imagine I go hunting for him. I find him at his house, changing into clothes that don't make sense. Me, convincing him to go to another part of the river where there is no bridge, where we could break off hunks of the Apple Jack and feel the buzz in our heads when the tobacco gets wet in our mouths and the two of us trying not to throw up. Him, going home at the end of the afternoon, miles from any bridges.

"So you know you couldn't have done anything to stop this, right?" he says. I should wait before I talk, but I don't. "I won't ever know that," I say. "Yes, you will," my father says. "All you need is a place to go and think it through. You can come here, if you want." He isn't looking at me. Instead, he's watching his toes dig little trenches in the warm, dry sand. "You should take a swim," he says. "Go ahead."

I wonder if he brought my swimsuit in the car, if he thought that far ahead. "Take off your uniform," he says. "You get that thing wet, it might shrink or turn colors or something, and your mother will have my ass."

A swim would feel good, I think. I peel off my Kingstree Manufacturing uniform and lay it on the sand next to the socks. Number 11, my favorite number. The ragged little hole on the back of the pants from sliding wrong. I steal bases. Lonnie is too slow. Was too slow. I consider leaving on my underwear, then think about how wet it will be later on and peel them off too. I don't mind being naked in front of my father. Not the first time, but he isn't even looking at me. His eyes are closed and pointed toward the sun. I wade into the black water and feel it close around my shins. It still has a chill to it, even in early June. I walk a little farther and feel the quiet current tugging at me like a rope is around my waist and some-body downstream is pulling. Lonnie's body drifted almost a quarter mile from the bridge. It took three days for the sheriff's department to find him. I think about the way bodies drift, even in June water, low June water. Instead of anchoring my toes in the sand and mud, I let my feet go and lay back in the water, the black closing over me.

Before my head goes under, I hear my father say, "Don't get out of sight. Stay where I can see you." But he doesn't have to worry about me forgetting where I am.

ACKNOWLEDGEMENTS

LOVE AND APPRECIATION TO MY GIRLS, Emily Gould and Maggie Gould, the better storytellers. Thanks to my fishing pal and father, Jack Gould. Exponential thanks to Betsy Teter and Meg Reid at Hub City Press for caring. For the early push, thanks to Vera Sullivan and Ella Sharpe. Thanks (and a toast skyward) to departed teachers James Dickey and William Price Fox. Also many thanks to Wilton Barnhardt, Karen Brennan, David Shields and Pete Turchi. Early, patient (and constant) reader, Ashley Landess, deserves appreciation and a medal. The Pack (Larry Bingham, Jynne Martin, Paula Belnap and Diane Arieff) have always provided motivation, wise counsel and laughs—thanks, guys. Thanks to Dale Ray Phillips for *My People's Waltz*. Thanks to my students, friends and colleagues at the S.C. Governor's School for the Arts and Humanities, especially Mamie Morgan and Alan Rossi. To the editors at the literary magazines who published some of these stories, I really appreciate the kind consideration. Thanks to George Singleton for the kick(s) in the ass. Thanks to the S.C. Arts Commission for fellowship support. A special thanks to the good folks of Kingstree, S.C., past and present. And to Shannon, I can't possibly thank you enough. But I'll try.

SCOTT GOULD'S work has appeared in
the *Kenyon Review, Carolina Quarterly, New Ohio
Review, Black Warrior Review, New Madrid Journal,*
and *New Stories from the South,* among others. He is a
past winner of the Literature Fellowship from the South
Carolina Arts Commission and the Fiction Fellowship
from the South Carolina Academy of Authors.

WWW.SCOTTGOULDWRITER.COM | @SCOTT_GOULD

HUB CITY PRESS

HUB CITY PRESS is a non-profit independent press in Spartanburg, SC, that publishes well-crafted, high-quality works by new and established authors, with an emphasis on the Southern experience. We are committed to high-caliber novels, short stories, poetry, plays, memoir, and works emphasizing regional culture and history. We are particularly interested in books with a strong sense of place.

Hub City Press is an imprint of the non-profit Hub City Writers Project, founded in 1995 to foster a sense of community through the literary arts. Our metaphor of organization purposely looks backward to the nineteenth century when Spartanburg was known as the "hub city," a place where railroads converged and departed.

RECENT HUB CITY PRESS TITLES

Flight Path: A Search for Roots beneath the World's Busiest Airport • Hannah Palmer

Over the Plain Houses • Julia Franks

Suburban Gospel • Mark Beaver

Minnow • James E. McTeer II

Pasture Art • Marlin Barton

Punch. • Ray McManus

The Whiskey Baron • Jon Sealy

The Only Sounds We Make • Lee Zacharias